I0669072

THE BELLS

THE BELLS

‡

A NOVEL

Cai Emmons

 Red Hen Press | *Pasadena, CA*

The Bells
Copyright © 2025 by the Estate of Cai Emmons
All Rights Reserved

No part of this book may be used or reproduced in any manner whatsoever without the prior written permission of both the publisher and the copyright owner. Publisher expressly prohibits the use of this work in connection with the development of any software program, including, without limitation, training a machine learning or generative artificial intelligence (AI) system.

Book layout by Ava Morgan

Library of Congress Cataloging-in-Publication Data

Names: Emmons, Cai author
Title: The bells: a novel / Cai Emmons.
Description: First edition. | Pasadena, CA: Red Hen Press, 2025.
Identifiers: LCCN 2025022726 (print) | LCCN 2025022727 (ebook) |
   ISBN 9781636283623 paperback | ISBN 9781636284354 library binding |
   ISBN 9781636283630 ebook
Subjects: LCGFT: Novels | Fiction
Classification: LCC PS3605.M57 B45 2025 (print) | LCC PS3605.M57 (ebook)
   | DDC 813/.6—dc23/eng/20250606
LC record available at https://lccn.loc.gov/2025022726
LC ebook record available at https://lccn.loc.gov/2025022727

The National Endowment for the Arts, the Los Angeles County Arts Commission, the Ahmanson Foundation, the Dwight Stuart Youth Fund, the Max Factor Family Foundation, the Pasadena Tournament of Roses Foundation, the Pasadena Arts & Culture Commission and the City of Pasadena Cultural Affairs Division, the City of Los Angeles Department of Cultural Affairs, the Audrey & Sydney Irmas Charitable Foundation, the Meta & George Rosenberg Foundation, the Albert and Elaine Borchard Foundation, the Adams Family Foundation, Amazon Literary Partnership, the Sam Francis Foundation, and the Mara W. Breech Foundation partially support Red Hen Press.

First Edition
Published by Red Hen Press
www.redhen.org

For Miriam

THE BELLS

For a while we lived with people,
but we saw no sign in them of the faithfulness we wanted.
It's better to hide completely within
as water hides in metal, as fire hides in a rock.

—Rumi

Bells are meant to remind us that God alone is good, that
we belong to Him, that we are not living for this world.
They break in upon our cares in order to remind us that
all things pass away and that our preoccupations are not
important.

—Thomas Merton, *Thoughts in Solitude*

PART ONE

1

All the other brothers were worshipping at the chapel when his mother came to fetch him. He had said goodbye to a few of the men individually, exchanging cordial but formal handshakes. He could see they pitied him. *We'll miss you,* a few of them said. The Abbot had embraced him and said a few generically pious words. But when the final hour came and he heard the car advancing up the driveway, he hefted his small duffle and walked out alone. It was midday, late June, hot and humid. His footsteps, unstable on the crunchy gravel, felt rude against the backdrop of the muffled solo voice reaching him from the chapel, the sound of a life receding. Other voices rose like a soaring flock of birds to join the soloist, Joseph—eighty-two years old and he still sang with a rich soulful voice that conveyed the accumulated wisdom of all his years. Niall couldn't hear the words, but he knew them by heart, "*O God, our true life, to know you is life, to serve you is perfect freedom . . .*" A few chickens foraging on the lawn clucked; otherwise there was only the droning silence of a long summer day that would drag on forever if you had failed to adequately know and love God.

He had pictured a moment of departure with a gaggle of brothers crowding around to wish him well, a ritual that would have been a proper demarcation of the end of something. But to leave without any well-wishing underscored his failure. He was a man who had, after five years, not learned to commit. A man who couldn't endure the contemplative ascetic life. A man who had performed religiosity instead of living it honestly. Worse, much worse, he was a man with an ugly mark of hate on his soul. None of the brothers would have said this aloud, but Niall suspected they held this view.

He and his mother—what gratitude he felt in her presence, what shame—rode in silence down the long driveway. She hadn't wanted him to join in the first place, but she'd supported his decision, and now he'd disappointed her for failing to persevere. It was the second professional choice he had failed to make good on, the first an aborted PhD in history. One of the cows had come close to the wire fence, and she watched them with her dilated eyes, bidding him a mournful goodbye as if she knew exactly what was happening and was happy not to be in his shoes.

As they exited past the stone gateposts onto the main road, heading east for Boston, he waited for elation—at the very least relief—but he felt nothing, and as farmland ceded to gas stations and strip malls, depression misted over him.

2

Niall cuts a circuitous path down the corridor through the snarl of students. A month into his new teaching job and he still gets queasy before every class. The hysteria of the hallway lodges itself in his gut, and he carries it into the classroom, feeling its continuing churn as he teaches. Music blaring from phones. Locker doors slamming. Students leaping and shrieking and flinging their nubile limbs. He's only thirty-three, still reasonably young and nimble enough to dodge the roadblocks, but he can't avoid the pungent smell of these adolescent bodies or the glimpses of so many half-exposed breasts and bellies. The students command the school's hallways so he's mostly invisible; even in his classroom his visibility is sometimes in question. A year and a few months out of the monastery, he still isn't used to the world's clatter, but it's better to be here than hibernating in his mother's spare room.

He's a misfit here, a white, middle-class history teacher of Irish descent in a New Jersey high school whose student population is working class and sixty-percent black and brown. But this is where he has chosen to be, hoping he might make some difference and finally learn to be good. The school has lofty ambitions to open doors for these kids, and Niall hopes working with young people, especially struggling young people, might be a way to redeem himself. But only a month into teaching he already wonders if he's the right person to be facilitating such door-opening. Not only is he a neophyte in the outside world himself, he's also cowed by most of his students. Their energy. Their youth and beauty. Their strong opinions. He's far too timid to be standing in front of a class instructing skeptical adolescents about the past. He can't shake the memory of his older brother Liam taunting him throughout childhood for being a fraidy-cat.

He has just had his second lunch with Trinity White, a science teacher, also new this year, the youngest teacher at the school. She's a recent Princeton graduate, formidable for her physics degree and her height—over six feet—and for the way she remains aloof from the other faculty members. He watched her in the meetings before school began, intimidated by her confidence but drawn to her as a fellow newcomer and someone who, like him, keeps to herself. In a faculty of fifty, she's one of only seven teachers of color. She stands out not only for her stature, but also for her mode of dressing: pencil skirts and tailored jackets, pantyhose and low pumps, so different from the casual sartorial style of the other teachers who wear pants and T-shirts, even hoodies. At some point, in talking to his girlfriend Lluvia, it occurred to him that Trinity's aloofness was not superiority but self-doubt equal to his own. He thought they could be allies, but he had no idea how to make that happen. "Invite her for lunch," Lluvia suggested. But he resisted. "Wouldn't such an invitation appear to be a romantic overture?" Lluvia laughed. "How many people conduct their dates in a high school lunchroom?" She was right, but it still took Niall over a week to summon the bravery to initiate lunch. Since he and Trinity don't naturally cross paths, he had to stop by her classroom and, though he'd practiced his invitation line beforehand, it still came out sounding dorky. "I'd like to offer you an invitation to lunch?" It wasn't a question, but in his delivery, it sounded like one. "In the lunchroom," he clarified. He had been similarly hamstrung in asking Lluvia out, watching and chatting with her for weeks at Starbucks before he made his move. It turned out that she was planning to ask *him* if he didn't get moving.

The first lunch with Trinity was horribly awkward. The faculty lunchroom was full and noisy, and Trinity's hushed voice was hard to hear. Niall was embarrassed by his Tupperware container of gloppy, week-old chili; Trinity was eating a turkey and cheese sandwich that looked as if it had been cut with the aid of a ruler. He wasn't a slob, not really, but he felt like one. Ten years her senior, he thought he should take the conversational reins, not his forte, so he began to speak about recent rumors he'd heard from other teachers, things that had been worrying him about the school's dysfunction: the bullying, the intransigent racial factions, the difficulty keeping a principal on board for more than two or three years. She stopped eating to regard him, impassive, a possibly wry upturn at one corner of her mouth.

"I was a student here myself not that many years ago," she said.

"You're kidding?"

"I'm not."

What a dope he was. "It's only hearsay. I'm only repeating what I've overheard. Incurable eavesdropper, you know? I'm sure it can't all be true," he said, backpedaling, wishing he'd conveyed more optimism.

"No worries." She seemed amused by him.

She told him about her brief teacher training—like his, it hadn't taught her much that wasn't instinctive—and about her physics studies at Princeton—her senior research paper called "Synthesis and Characterization of Zinc Oxide Thin-Films for Similar Band Gap Material Junctions"—and he realized he was right to be intimidated by her. At the end of the lunch, feeling a need to show her he wasn't a complete slouch, he blurted out that he'd spent five years in a monastery, a topic he rarely raised himself.

She elevated one eyebrow. "The plot thickens. This merits another lunch." Such a small movement, that eyebrow, but it archived an entire vocabulary of humor.

At today's lunch—he'd brought a neat cheese sandwich cut crosswise to match hers—she was eager to hear about the monastery. What had prompted him to join? Naivete, his standard answer, along with an absence of any other calling. And why did he leave? His inability to speak to God, to pray, or in the end, feel certain of God's existence, which made him feel like an imposter. The larger story, the more complete and honest version, is too complicated for a school lunchroom.

"The idea of God has always seemed laughable to me," she said. "Wishful thinking. I'm sorry—I hope I'm not offending you. At college, everyone was declaring themselves instant Buddhists—religion of the month, it made me sick."

"I'm not offended. I'm a secular guy these days. But what about your name? Isn't Trinity . . . ?"

"My mother's all in with religion. Which is probably why I'm not. Don't you regret having spent those years away from the world?"

"Yes and no. I learned things I might not have learned out here."

She raised an eyebrow. "More fodder for future conversations. I'd find it impossible. I'd miss so much. TV, music, movies, fashion. I'd have terrible FOMO."

"FOMO?"

"You really have been a shut-in, haven't you? Fear of missing out. What did you miss the most?"

"I've never been a big talker, but the other brothers were right there and you're discouraged from talking to them unless it's necessary. I wanted to know where they came from and what their lives were like before they joined the monastery. I thought when I got out, I'd want to talk and talk and talk, but now I'd be happy doing a lot less talking."

"You don't need to talk to me."

"Not this kind of talking. I like this. But teaching—all the blather, you know? I hate to say it, but I'm not really built for teaching." It felt good to say it aloud. "Please don't tell anyone."

She laughed. "Who would I tell? You humanities people. Those of us in the sciences keep our speechifying to a minimum." She paused to assess him. "Anyway, you seem to be doing fine so far."

"You wouldn't say that if you saw me teaching."

It was good, talking to Trinity—he looks forward to more. He walked her to her classroom, trying to channel some of her confidence to help him through his next class, noting the inquisitive glances of some of the other teachers as they left the lunchroom. He needs to mention his girlfriend to Trinity so she doesn't get the wrong idea, but he isn't sure how to do so organically. Interpersonal protocols remain a mystery to him.

"Have a good afternoon," he said before diving into the current of students.

"Hey, Mr. O! Looks like you got yourself a girlfriend!"

It's Jayden, from his next class, a genial guy who never shuts up, yammering throughout the fifty-minute period. Niall laughs rather than refute Jayden, as refutation seems like confirmation, and the last thing Niall needs is Jayden spreading a false rumor.

He stops by the men's room to take a leak. It's empty—he's going to be late for class. As he pisses, he thinks of Trinity White's impassive face, her single raised eyebrow. Did she train her face to be so still, or is it that way naturally? He told her half-truths today, and it bothers him. But to tell the full story takes time and a receptive, non-judgmental listener, and he hardly knows Trinity White. He hasn't even told Lluvia the full story.

Speaking about the monastery never fails to transport him back. There were unpleasant things that transpired, but there was so much else. The luminous silence. Rising at 3:00 a.m., stepping from his room onto the grounds, sniffing, the dark air pressing into him, lifting him as he walked to prayers, everything at that hour alive with mystery. The unlit path bordered the cow pasture where one or two cows would low in gentle greeting. The musk of their warm bodies flared his nostrils to mirror theirs. The light tapping of the other brothers' footsteps arriving, a few of the oldest ones with shuffling gaits. Robes chuffing as they filed through the chapel door, nodding, taking their seats in the pews. He worked and prayed next to those gentle men, elbow to elbow, shoulder to shoulder, developing an impersonal intimacy. He felt such fellowship with them and yet they conversed so rarely.

Silence shimmered beneath the sounds of the daily devotional work. The clattering vats they used for cheese-making. The snipping shears and snapping branches as he pruned the rose bushes, the hydrangeas, the lilacs. The gritty claw of the rake. Even the mower and tractor contained silence beneath their thrashing. And an even more profound silence was woven among the bells summoning them to prayers. In the basso profundo of their plainsong, the Gregorian fourths and fifths. The voices blending, rising, falling, dolorous, ecstatic. When the chanting ended, an attenuated aftermath of intervals and grace notes echoed along the corridors and through the courtyards and over the lawn and garden and pasture, finally fading into a monumental silence that reminded them all of their insignificant place in the universe.

What a contrast the silence of that place is to where he has landed, here on the roiling coastline of New Jersey, most of his waking hours spent in the cacophony of an American public high school.

3

As he expected, he's late to his post-lunch class, the class that, from the beginning, has been his bumpiest and most interesting. His other four classes have gone mostly according to plan; the students don't seem excited by the history he's teaching them, but luckily, except for a few individuals, they're too lazy or bored to resist. The strong personalities in this class, however, bounce off one another and make every meeting unpredictable. And because they meet after lunch, they're pumped with caloric energy, most of it from sugar.

The students don't notice him entering; for a moment, he's a fly on the wall. The view is something Hieronymus Bosch would have delighted in painting: bodies bending every-which-way, gum balls soaring, several girls fixing each other's hair. So much youthful piss-and-vinegar. It would be funny were he not in charge of taming them.

"Mr. O—you're late!" Jayden yells, winking. "You got the hots for Ms. White?"

Niall makes his way to the haven of his desk without responding. Jayden isn't malicious—in fact he's one of Niall's favorites—but Niall makes a note to ask him to back off. The challenge of arriving late is reversing the momentum of their antics and resetting the atmosphere. Their energy is nuclear, sometimes frightening. He's fond of them—most of them—if only he didn't feel so helpless in their presence. And he faults himself for already having favorites.

He's been guiding them slowly through the prescribed curriculum that covers the Civil War and Reconstruction to the present day. They're moving much too slowly; after a month they haven't gotten past the Gettysburg Address, today's topic. He glances down at his notes, his mind veering to Trinity White again. He's pretty sure she would corral these students more readily than he can. He'd love to have her height, accompanied by authority—at five feet, six inches he feels compromised. He's been trying to work on raising his voice, aware he usually speaks too softly. The music from Dominic's phone plays on, the lyrics in Spanish, the reverb haunting. Jayden and Rania are hip-bumping, the sight so baldly sexual Niall turns away. Colton and Anthony are arm wrestling at one of the tables. Colton comes from a wealthy family and has the enviably buff physique of a wrestler which he loves to flaunt by wearing tight pants and spandex shirts, usually black. Rumors abound about him, and it's not hard to see why—he moves around the school like a surly prince so even the faculty who don't teach him know who he is. The story goes that he arrived at the school in the middle of the last year, having been kicked out—flunked out?—of three private schools. It's hard to understand how he ended up here, as his parents surely don't live in this working-class coastal town. He disdains everything about the school, but he's gathered a following among some of the white kids. Niall doesn't understand why. Is it his wealth? His physique? His disdain? Something impresses those kids, but nothing about Colton has made a hit with Niall.

"Okay, Dominic, cut the music."

"Aww, Mr. O."

"Cut it." His raised voice, which isn't his habit, causes several students to turn in his direction.

Dominic complies, and when Jayden and Rania, who both

command a power of their own, take their seats, the chaos subsides a bit. "Hey, Mr. O," Jayden calls. "We wanna see you dance. Can we have a dance party?" Niall can't discern if Jayden is being affectionate or goading. Perhaps a bit of both.

"I'm no dancer, I promise you."

"We'll show you. You can bring Miss White. I bet she likes to dance."

"Maybe at the end of the term. But now, Colton, Anthony, this isn't gym class."

The boys remain latched, hands in a tight grip, lips clenched, eyes slitted. They are a power center too magnetic for Niall to compete with. Colton wears his signature black cap backwards, a slab of blond hair emerging like a pelt to cover his neck. Anthony's head is shaved. The crowns of their heads face off like hornless bulls. Something is at stake here and the class senses it, all eyes on the two boys who have hitherto acted as friends. Colton is on the wrestling team which supposedly makes him better than everyone else in the class, but Anthony appears to be a credible challenger. Both boys' arms remain straight up, neither budging a millimeter. Niall could try to insist they stop, but he knows they won't, and he can't waste precious capital on such a request.

"Italian Stallion vs. Moneybags," Jayden narrates, mimicking a sportscaster. "Two white dudes lookin' to take each other down. Place your bets, folks. Who's gonna win?"

Colton's face puffs, pinkens—clearly, he's mad. Some of the students clap. "Go. Go. Go." It isn't entirely clear who they're rooting for, but Niall senses their sympathies lie with underdog Anthony who's gaining an edge. Whatever is happening, the competition isn't friendly.

Colton mutters what is surely a profanity. Then, he's down. A sudden *thunk* as fist and arm crash on the table. "Fuck!" He shoves a book to the floor.

Anthony rises from his seat, raising his arms in victory and sauntering among the tables, led by his hips. "For real for real." He slaps the outstretched hands.

"Fucking Wop," Colton says, extending his middle finger at Anthony.

"Colton!" Niall warns.

The other students are more jazzed than ever now, excited by savage competition among two white guys who were supposedly friends. Niall listens in stillness for a moment, taking measure, weighing his plans. Snippets of conversation reach him: *I'm crying. Kiss my ass. No way, dude.* It's a vernacular Niall must quash or master. Every day is a balancing act. The Gettysburg Address, with its noble ideals and Old World cadences, isn't a good bet for this moment. *Think fast, Niall.*

Seized by a thought, inspired by Lluvia who is a whimsical but expert problem-solver, he spins, hoping to distract them. Round and round he goes, spreading his arms like a kid on a playground, the classroom blurring.

"Yo! You goin' crazy on us?" Jayden is laughing. The other students clap.

Niall stops himself, suddenly embarrassed—what did he think he was he doing?—vision quivering, stomach uncertain. But his uncharacteristic behavior has succeeded in galvanizing their attention. He swallows gastric acid and points at Aliyah. "Okay, Aliyah—pick three words from the Gettysburg Address."

Her eyes pop. She's theatrical, borderline hysterical. "What?"

"Choose three words, any words. If you don't have a copy, find a copy."

Rania hands Aliyah a hard copy.

"Any three words?"

"Any three words. Say them aloud."

She glances around at the other students, receives nothing, finally looks down at the paper. "Men?"

"Yes, okay. Two more."

"Four?"

"Yes . . . ?"

"Equal?"

"Okay, those are your three words. Write them down. Shannel, you're next. Three words. Different ones. Roman, you're after Shannel."

Niall is channeling someone else, possibly Trinity; this person barking orders is no one he's ever been before, but he's centered again and coming back to himself, wresting control. He proceeds around the room, calling to one student then another. Dutifully, they select their words—*Dead, Devotion, Course; Vain, God, Birth; People, Perish, Prosper.* They settle into the task, engaged for the moment, curious about why they're doing this. He arrives at Colton whose body is slack, a portrait of refusal.

"Come on, you're holding things up."

Colton sighs. "Is. Are. To."

"You can do better than that, Colton. Choose at least one significant word."

"You let Rania use little words."

"Yes, because she chose significant words—*of, by, for.* Come on, Colton, get with it."

Niall hears his voice has tipped past authority to harshness. He's unpleasantly aware of disliking Colton. Colton scans the room for support from someone, but the other students, caught up in the activity, are lost to him.

"Dead," Colton finally mutters. "World. Living."

"That's better."

They all have their words. *Whadya got?* they ask each other.

"Okay, now your job is to write song lyrics with your words. You can write to a tune you know if you want or, if you're musically inclined, you can make up a new tune. You can write about anything but try to reveal something about the state of the country. Or something important in your own life."

"I can't write a song!"

"Sure you can. You listen to songs all the time, don't you? Do what those songwriters do."

"What's the song s'posed to be *about*."

"As I said, anything. It doesn't have to be about history. But if you can, make it a meaningful statement of some kind."

"Is hip-hop okay?"

"Any style, any content. The only absolute requirement is that you use your three words. And no racial slurs or sex."

"Pop Smoke is okay?"

"Pop Smoke?"

"The singer, dude."

"Sure, whoever you want."

"I'm gonna do Beyoncé."

"Imma do Olivia Rodrigo!"

"Billie Eilish."

Niall shrugs. These names mean nothing to him.

"Can we use our phones? I gotta find my song."

"Phones are allowed, but only with ear buds and only as long as I can see you're really working. Now, get to it."

A few of the girls—Rania, Tiffany, Camilla—mobilize immediately, installing ear buds, scrolling, scribbling. It isn't long before everyone follows. Jayden breaks into falsetto: "Gonna write me a song. An A-mer-i-can bal-lad! Springsteen, kiss your Jersey ass goodbye."

"Okay, Jayden, get to work."

"I *am* working. I'm singing, like you said to do."

"Yes, but keep it down."

Mateo, the sweet, perpetually dazed student with the hare lip, appears befuddled, but even he is listening to something. Colton has put in ear buds. He slouches in his seat, legs stretched beneath the table, eyes closed. After fifteen minutes he hasn't picked up his pen. Niall, suspecting Colton has no intention of writing anything, wanders to his table and taps his shoulder.

"Wake up, Colton."

Colton jerks to attention. "Wha'?"

Niall, vision blurred, seizes one of Colton's ear buds and brings it to his own ear. It's blasting noise—if there's a melody underneath the mayhem, Niall can't hear it.

"Hey, man, give that back. What's wrong with you?"

"Do you plan to write your lyrics to this music?"

"Maybe."

"Well, get to work."

"This is bullshit. This isn't history. We're supposed to be learning history." Colton's words are thick with saliva as if he might spit.

"This is your assignment, Colton. Get to work."

"Stop picking on me."

Niall returns to his desk, trying to relax and appreciate his larger accomplishment: Everyone but Colton is writing something. Niall has no idea *what* they're writing and whether he will be able to relate their work to American history, but he has time to work that out. Meanwhile, he's proud of himself for focusing their interest, and he can't let Colton ruin this. *What's wrong with you?* He closes his eyes and sends up a quick prayer, trying to invoke advice from his chosen mentor, Thomas Merton. "It is necessary that I be human and remain human."

He surveys his students, heads nodding to various beats, a few of them scribbling. They're not talking to each other, surely a first. This might be the best moment of teaching he has had so far. If only Colton weren't casting a shadow; even in his silence he remains a whole-body irritant; sure of his superiority, he is a too-familiar type that never fails to destabilize Niall. Niall cautions himself: He must not let annoyance solidify into hatred.

4

The sulphureous smell of the ocean is especially pungent tonight as Niall drives through the quiet back streets of town on his way to Lluvia's. He will be meeting her mother and daughter for the first time, so of course he is nervous. He wonders if it's too soon—he's only known Lluvia since the beginning of summer.

It took a month of flirting at Starbucks before Niall dared to ask her out. They were both there at ten o'clock every morning, she on her work break, he prepping his upcoming classes. They exchanged meaningful glances across tables, which led to cheerful comments lobbed from table to table, which led to her coming to his table where they chitchatted—her standing, him sitting—about her job as a physical therapist, his upcoming job as a teacher. After a week of these awkward sitting-standing exchanges, they finally escalated to sharing a table. Then, during a heat wave in early July, the air so thickened with moisture it felt like work to walk through it, he finally asked her to join him for a stroll on the beach. Beside him Lluvia skipped and skittered and bounced across the sand. Hair damp, face flushed, she appeared unbothered by the heat. They followed the water line and occasionally she ran ahead of him and spun, energized by the briny scent of the breeze.

She showered him with questions, apologizing for being so forward. A little younger than he—thirty to his thirty-three—

she'd already racked up impressive life experience. In Puerto Rico, where she was born and raised, she'd gotten pregnant at eighteen. She married the man, but he left her when Flora was still a baby. She and Flora and her mother Rocio then relocated to the US where Lluvia earned her college degree, studied to become a physical therapist, and found a job, all while mothering Flora. Despite these challenges—or was it because of them?—she had retained the eager mien of a young girl. She didn't even express resentment toward the man who'd deserted her, claiming to be better off for it.

Riveted by her cheerful aura and her lightly accented speech, he tried to ignore the glare of the sun and the sand in his shoes and the occasional gusts of wind that made it hard to hear her. He liked the beach—it was on a beach that he'd decided to enter the monastery—but his favorite landscape was a serene inland lake.

They walked for a mile or so then stopped to remove their shoes. He rolled up his pant legs, and they waded into the water, allowing the small waves to lick their shins. The shallow water was surprisingly warm. She took his hand as if they were school kids.

"Do you like to swim? I love to swim. I would have loved to be a mermaid."

He laughed. There *was* a touch of the mermaid about her. Yes, he said, he knew how to swim. His mother had insisted he and his brother Liam learn, but he'd never sought the activity for anything other than cooling off. Lluvia, it was obvious, liked swimming for its own sake.

They gazed out at the minimalist view before them, equal bands of ocean and sky, New York's skyline a barely discernible blip on the horizon to the north, and the skin of the world expanded around them, tugging and nudging them with its largesse.

"How about we swim tomorrow?" she suggested.

"Why not?" he said, feeling adventurous for a change and ready to do whatever she suggested. He would come to recognize this as her favorite phrase: *How about?* A plunge into possibility. An experiment with the unknown. *How about we swim, move in together, marry, make a baby?* She wasn't constricted, as he was, by worries about how things might unfold.

She had to get back to work, but they made a plan to swim the next day in the early evening. He had nothing to swim in. The store he went to carried only trunks with stars or polka dots or American flags or sea creatures, intended, no doubt, for people more like his students. Too lazy to go elsewhere, he chose a turquoise pair, decorated with purple octopuses, an uncomfortably flashy choice for him, but they delighted Lluvia.

She had brought a picnic supper packed by her mother—*So much food!* they both said, laughing, knowing they would eat little. Bread and cheese and deli meats and cookies and apples. They walked as far as they could from the omnipresent crowds, laid down towels and the picnic basket, and stripped their outer clothes down to bathing suits. The pallor of his un-muscled torso embarrassed him, but she, already heading to the water, barely glanced in his direction. Her taut, full, bikini-clad bottom swung gently from side to side, and he tried not to stare. Reaching the water, she waded in—no hesitation, no shrieking, no attention-seeking histrionics he associated with women and water. When she was up to her waist she ducked under and stroked out, her brown arms rhythmic, the disturbed water around her making rainbows of the evening light. He was so drawn to her confidence, her independence, so impressed by the elegance of her sinuous stroke, that he dove in without delay and made his way out to her as quickly as he could in his flapping freestyle. She treaded water and laughed at him, and he took her into his arms, smitten. They both went under and came up laughing. Everything about her embodied the goodness and joy he'd been seeking.

On the surface, Lluvia doesn't resemble his mother at all. His mother is large and composed and holds her thoughts to herself;

Lluvia is small and restlessly alive, emotions trickling from every part of her quick body. But their effect on him is similar, almost tranquilizing. When he was really young, maybe preverbal, he would nestle into his mother's lap and the sound of her voice, reading to him, rippled through him like water, sending him into a liminal state in which he was alert to all his senses while seemingly asleep. It was a state he later associated with proximity to God.

Lluvia's house is only a few miles from his own, in the same working-class coastal New Jersey town where he teaches. Rocio, Lluvia's mother, barely five feet tall, pulls Niall into her plush bosom, chuckling as she does so. Startled, he squeezes back gamely. Their modest ranch house exudes contentment, the living room furnished with well-used furniture, a threadbare beige sofa, faintly stained blue floral carpeting, the sliding door to the patio pockmarked with dust and globs of white bird poop. Some of the clutter has been dumped into catch-all baskets or shoved under the coffee table in a last-minute sweep. But Niall appreciates that it's mostly what he would consider "good" clutter: books and magazines, a recorder and loose sheet music, a pad of construction paper and masking tape, a screwdriver, a hammer, a bag of nails. The stuff of engaged living that makes Niall ashamed of his own Spartan apartment. The aroma of roasting pork permeates everything. Niall can't remember the last time he ate pork.

He sits at the head of the table where he's been told to sit, savoring the hedonistic pleasure of it all. Home-cooked Puerto Rican food—*pernil asado,* Lluvia tells him, pork shoulder, along with rice and beans. Chatter. Family life. The kind of creature comforts he was trained for so long to reject. His own childhood by contrast was restrained, his electrician father and librarian mother both introverts; Liam, now a lawyer, was the only one who talked much. And living with the brothers at the monastery was intimate, but not personal. They worked in close physical proximity but knew nothing of each other's inner lives.

The meat is so tender it falls from the bone. The rice and beans are seasoned with some fragrant herb he doesn't recognize. He wonders if they eat meals this good every day—he could get used to this. He's been living the clichéd life of a bachelor—or perhaps the cliché of a former monk—in a one-bedroom apartment with minimal furniture and bare walls, a kitchenette in the living room rather than a full kitchen, one-dish meals prepared on Sunday that last him the entire week. It's not that he prefers it that way, but it hasn't occurred to him to devote time to dressing things up and cooking more frequently. The truth is, as with grocery shopping, he has never really learned how. When Lluvia comes for an overnight—neither of them feels comfortable having an overnight at her house with daughter and mother so proximate— she laughs at the cheerlessness of his place and often brings flowers to brighten it. He's begun to make a few purchases: better pillows, new sheets, a comforter.

Twelve-year-old Flora watches him with the same wariness as some of his students. Lluvia has confessed that in the last year Flora has become challenging. Wiry and flat-chested, with the same full face and brown curls of her mother and grandmother, she's still a girl, but her outfit of spandex leggings and black T-shirt with a cut-out around the belly button tells him she's barreling toward adolescence. She exudes a cheerful sociability like Lluvia, but it's wrapped around a dare. *Don't ask about school*, was the first thing she said to him when they were introduced. *Grownups always ask about school and it's so boring. Also, unoriginal.* She had his number. What else do you ask a child of twelve?

"Were you, like, a real monk in robes and everything?"

He laughs. "Yup. The works."

"You don't *look* like a monk."

"How do monks look?"

"I don't know—beards and serious faces. Always praying and shit. Why would you want to be a monk?"

"Flora," Lluvia warns. *"No seas grosera."*

"It's okay," he says. "I ask myself the same thing. But I was pretty young when I decided—not that that's an excuse."

"Now he teaches history," Rocio tells Flora in her Puerto Rican-accented English. She is in her early fifties, he guesses, a little younger than his own mother.

"O-M-G. I hate history. History teaches you that human beings weren't any better back then than they are now. Always fucking up from the moment we stopped being apes."

"Flora, watch your language," Lluvia says. Rocio shakes her head indulgently.

"Well, it's true. Our teacher said there's, like, only twelve years in human history when there wasn't any war going on."

Niall nods. "Sometimes human beings act nobly."

"Yeah, right. There's some really noble behavior in my school. Yesterday, some asshole dumped his soda on the lunch tray of one of the CP kids on purpose. You know, a kid in a wheelchair."

"I hope someone did something," Lluvia says.

"Someone got the kid another tray, but the kid who did it, Dylan—he got away with it. No one said anything to him. *Nada.* At least not that I could see. So, yeah, I don't see many people acting nobly in my middle school life."

Niall wonders if such an action would be punished in his own school. Probably not. Too few people would notice.

Rice pudding for dessert. Indecently good. He isn't used to so much food, is much too full, but he finishes it anyway, in gratitude. He feels trapped. He feels happy. He doesn't know what he feels.

As he departs, Rocio embraces him again, holding him an extra second so he's suffused with the rhythm of her breathing. She pats his back as if he's her son. *"Eres un buen hombre."* His own mother's hugs are always brief.

Flora watches them from a distance, territorial, cat-like.

Lluvia follows him out to the stoop and shuts the door behind them. There's a hum from the main thoroughfare blocks away, but otherwise the night is quiet in this residential neighborhood, not surprising for a weeknight. The autumn air is bracingly cool, a feeling he associates with expectation. A single skateboarder inscribes wide parabolas down the center of the street, their elegance at odds with the grating scrape of wheels on asphalt.

"Thank you," he says. "They're both wonderful."

"Give Flora a few years and she'll be more wonderful. *Si Dios quiere.*"

"Oh, I think she's pretty great right now."

"Don't you think we should think about living together? Get married?"

A simple question without a prologue that lofts out into the still autumn night. Did he hear her right?

"Marry?"

"Maybe you haven't heard of that. It's when two people decide . . ." She stands in front of him and takes his hands, chuckling. "You and me. Together."

"I wasn't expecting this."

"Yes, you were. Of course you were!"

She's right. He didn't admit it to himself, but why else did she invite him here tonight to meet her mother and daughter? *Say yes*, he tells himself. But he can't. He's only known her for a few months, and he has shown himself to be bad at commitment. He has already met the rotten center of his soul, though he can't possibly tell her that.

"I need to think about it."

"I knew we'd get married the moment I met you."

"How could you have thought that?"

"Call me psychic. *Soy bruja!*" She laughs.

"I wouldn't make a good husband."

"Don't be ridiculous. You're the best man I've ever met even if *you* don't know that. You can take your time to decide, but don't use that as an excuse! My mother obviously loves you and Flora will too."

"Not yet she doesn't."

"She will. I know her. But no rush. I'm not pressuring you. *Buenas noches.*"

She slips back inside without pausing for a kiss. He has offended her. When he reaches his car he glances back at the house, warm yellow light pulsing from its windows, a cornucopia of comfort. A ready-made family. In marrying Lluvia he would be a lone man among three women. Without refuge. Women notice things that most men fail to see.

Sometime after midnight he awakens from a nightmare. He's strangling Brother Thomas with his bare hands. Thomas's face is puffing, reddening, about to pop. Like Colton's face when he was wrestling.

He gets out of bed and goes to the kitchen for a glass of water, then wanders to the living room which looks out to the street where an invasive streetlight shoots unwelcome rays of orange into his living room. He can't believe he's still having these dreams, but they surface every few months from some cesspool in his brain. The feeling is still there. Festering.

If it weren't for Brother Thomas he might still be in the Massachusetts monastery, his days governed by the metronomic regularity of chanting, study, work in the gardens, milking, cheese-making, kneading bread, living side by side with those men in silence, often so close that the heat of the other men's bodies would seep through their woolen robes, traveling from man to man, building a collective energy. An electric force more powerful than anything he'd known before.

5

The summer after he left the monastery, he lived in a stupor of shame and inertia in the spare room of his mother's place in Arlington, near Boston, where she'd moved after Niall's father Glen died three years earlier. It was smaller than the spacious, if shabby, apartment in Charlestown where he'd grown up, but more upscale, with cherry woodwork and polished parquet floors. She had made it her own, hanging her historical photographs of Boston on the walls, spreading every spare surface with her collection of hand-painted porcelain teacups collected from garage sales she frequented, the shelves full of the old books she prized, bound in leather with marbled frontispieces, rescued from people who didn't value them as she did, a librarian and history buff. Now that her immediate family was gone, and she was still working, she had discretionary funds to spend on such things.

It wasn't Niall's home, and he was uncomfortable everywhere except for the single bed in the spare room where he remained for twelve to fourteen hours, sleeping fitfully then waking and thinking in repetitive loops, tortured and comforted by dream-like memories. Much of the time, he yearned to be back in the soothing shelter of the monastery surrounded by the tranquil rhythms, the activity of every hour prescribed. He could hear his mother getting ready for work at the other end of the apartment, the sound of cabinets opening and closing in the kitchen, the respectful tap of her shoes on the uncarpeted wooden floors. He always half-expected her to come into his room and wake him, but she never did. Her instructive practices were subtle, and they didn't include shaming. But he was good enough at shaming himself. He always knew the exact moment she was gone, the sudden absence of sound waves, the settling of dust motes, the silence like a summons for him to get moving. But he had no idea what he was supposed to do, how to move past this moment of humiliation and failure. The thought of joining the outside world filled him with dread. He had never been a man of action like his brother Liam. While the monastery had held its challenges, it had been easy to live there. Too easy. Its ritualized schedule told him exactly what to do and when. It was daunting to think there were many people here on the outside his own age, early thirties, who had already built full, multifaceted lives with careers and homes and families.

His mother urged him to eat with her, but he claimed not to be hungry. While she was at work, and after she'd gone to bed, he foraged quietly in the kitchen, eating things that didn't need cooking—cold cereal, yoghurt, nuts and dried fruit, sometimes uncooked spaghetti. Once a day he logged onto her computer in a corner of the living room to check in on the world. He'd never, even before the monastery, been wedded to a computer as many of his generation were; he used one only as a necessity as a graduate student. Now he was addled by what he found there in the news. A world he didn't recognize or understand, altered by a self-serving, mean-spirited president who had made things more chaotic and dangerous than before. Ten minutes of reading about politics was all he could take; then he would retreat to his bedroom again where he tried to read some of the biblical texts he'd failed to grasp in the monastery, without success. If he hadn't understood them in the monastery, he was never going to comprehend them on the outside. After a week, his mother, home from work, knocked on his door.

"If you're going to stay here a while, you need to begin pulling your own weight. I'm leaving you a shopping list for tomorrow. The supermarket is three blocks from here."

She lingered in the doorway until he nodded. All his life her composure had been remarkable, but he hadn't registered it fully until now, how her broad cheeks, remarkably smooth for a woman in her fifties, leaked nothing of her thoughts or feelings, her face as unrevealing as her bare belly or shoulder or foot would have been. Her strong opinions, which he knew she had, were stitched close to her, until she was ready to display them.

On the front hall table she had left him a shopping list, a stack of twenty-dollar bills, and an apartment key. It reminded him that he had no money of his own, another source of shame. He walked two blocks to the main road. Heat rose from the asphalt through the thin soles of his monastery slip-ons. Moving slowly, he felt like an elder or an invalid, a thin shoot of bamboo blown here and there by the passing traffic. The cars passed so fast it didn't seem as if real people were driving them. The pedestrians he encountered avoided his gaze, and he realized he shouldn't look at them either. But he caught glimpses of the stress deforming their faces and was sure he looked equally stressed. Sometimes he passed attractive women, and he looked away, overcome with the knowledge that he was now free to pursue women if he wanted. How could a man embrace desire again when he'd worked so hard against it?

In the supermarket parking lot, a man wearing a wool coat much too warm for summer was weaving among the cars, screaming. Niall couldn't understand the man's words. His gaping mouth looked predatory and he made Niall nervous, but everyone else was ignoring the man so Niall did too, trying to think of the peace of the cows in the monastery pasture. Their mild trusting curiosity, their unruffled stance.

The supermarket doors parted for him. Music was playing, light rock. He blinked against the assault of the overhead lights, green and buzzing, as he advanced into the store's bowels. A museum-like display of produce surrounded him, brightly colored and plastic-looking, too shiny to have grown in real dirt. He knew from the monastery how vegetables grew and what they looked like when harvested—not like this. The fruits and vegetables took up shelves that stretched to the back of the vast space. Who would eat all this? It looked like enough to feed the entire city of Boston. He pushed himself forward, for a moment recognizing the jaunty music coming from the loudspeakers though he wouldn't have been able to say what it was. It occurred to him to consult his mother's list. Potatoes, onions, garlic, carrots, spinach, tomatoes, lettuce, plums and peaches if they were any good. Bread, milk, coffee, tea, cookies. Lentils. Hamburger and chicken, sliced ham. It had been so long since he'd eaten meat. Growing up, he liked it, and he'd eaten it until he went into the monastery. There, all the meals had been vegetarian: rice and beans and vegetables.

He stood in front of the potato bins. Why had he never realized how many kinds of potatoes there were? Russets, Idaho, Red, Yellow, Fingerlings, Yukon Gold. He had no idea which ones to get, she hadn't specified. Why was there a need for so many different kinds of potatoes? He had never shopped for groceries alone, only with his mother or brother. When he was a history grad student, he had eaten mostly prepared food from delis. He watched the people around him choosing russets, so he took them too. He squeezed plums and peaches, testing for ripeness as others were doing. He tossed some into a bag without being sure of his choices. The same problem presented itself again and again: had there always been so many kinds of bread, cookies, tea? Oh, for a narrow life again, a life with few choices. He was already addled by decision overload. An announcement came over the loudspeaker—fourth of July picnic items were on sale in aisle four. The announcer's voice sounded panicked, the same voice he might use for an imminent bomb threat.

By the time he got to the checkout line he was skittish. He eyed the selections in his cart, hoping he had enough money, hoping he could fit everything into the two shopping bags she'd given him.

"Did you find everything you need?" the checkout woman said.

He nodded.

"How's your day going?"

Did she really care? The barcodes bleeped. The announcer came on again, this time plugging watermelon, as if people couldn't figure out on their own what they wanted. Music followed, an instrumental cover of a song by The Beatles. "Good Day Sunshine." He felt he might be an accidental actor in an avant-garde play. He imagined saying: *I'm a monk—they just released me.*

"Good. It's good. I'm good," he said.

The clerk squinted at him, as if he'd responded with the wrong line. "One twenty-seven even."

For a moment, her words seemed like code for something. Could she mean a hundred and twenty-seven dollars? He couldn't believe that two bags of food could cost that much. He peeled off seven of the twenties his mother had given him. Obviously, she knew how much groceries cost. The clerk counted change into his hand, and he pocketed it.

"Have a good day," she said, already eyeing her next customer.

This was the world now, he thought as he passed through the automatic doors. Maybe it had always been as indifferent as this. Were people still human, or had they been changed into robots while he was gone? It was absurd to see a single trip to the supermarket as a bellwether, to allow it to make him feel erased and irrelevant, but it had. He remembered, accurately or not, a different world, a kinder, more sensitive one. In the old neighborhood, strangers said hello to one another and even in his grad program, dysfunctional and mean-spirited as it was, people acknowledged one another.

Back at the apartment he unloaded the groceries and put them away. He thought he should make lentil soup for his mother—it was a dish he knew how to prepare, having done so many times in the monastery—but he didn't have the will. He retired to his room, lying on the bed. The brothers would be going to chapel now. He could almost hear them chanting, see them kneeling to pray. Afterwards, they would go to the dining hall for a simple one-dish meal that always satisfied. The chanting rose through his blood, an engorged river about to overflow, and he raised his voice to join them. *Kyrie eleison . . . Gloria in excelsis pacem.* But it wasn't the same, alone in his room, without the polyphony of the other brothers' voices.

He began to make himself leave the house every day on long walks to observe and acclimate to the world he'd reentered. Every day, seeing the people walk the streets with such determination struck him anew how ill-equipped he was for anything. To thrive in the world you needed so much—concrete things like money and a bank account, a computer, a cell phone, reputable clothing, an education, a resume. Then there were the intangible things, the confidence, the resourcefulness, the energy to propel yourself forward. He had the education, and curiosity, but he had regressed to feeling like a child, living with his mother like some ne'er-do-well, dependent on what she might give him to change his circumstances.

The summer dragged on, vampiric humidity sucking everyone dry. He began eating dinner with his mother, because she was being so good to him. He wanted to be good in return—it had always been his mission to be good, though how to do that was more of a challenge than he'd once thought it to be—and he tried to be a stimulating conversationalist, concealing his bleak outlook as well as he could. He urged her to talk about her day at work.

She was working at a special summer program for disadvantaged children and had heartwarming stories about children getting turned on to books.

"Have you thought about completing your PhD?" she asked him. "Or getting a social work degree? You'd be a good social worker, I think."

He could feel the slight tremor in her voice that spoke to her keen suppressed desire for him to get on with his life. He felt that same urgency, but his history of wrong choices haunted him. And he rued all he'd given up.

Several mass shootings happened that summer, one in Florida, one in Texas, one in Missoula, Montana. They dominated the news for a few days before people lost interest. He and his mother were both aware it was happening, but they chose not to discuss it. What was there to say? It was atrocious; there were too many guns in the country and too much bigotry and hatred, but neither of them could change that. And both of them believed, though they wouldn't necessarily have admitted to this, that people in the West and South were more given to violence than those in New England. They had both always thought Boston was too dignified for such things, but a massacre of seven at a Walmart a few towns away showed them they were wrong. No place was immune. It hit them both in the gut. He began to think these events might signify an important shift in human history, a rise in hostility, not just here in Boston but across the nation, even the world. History was full of such tipping points, but he had never lived through one. He knew they were prompted, most often, by scarcity, which led to hoarding, xenophobia, and eventually, war.

"Things seem to have changed in such a short time."

His mother sighed and laid down her soupspoon. They were eating the lentil soup he had finally made.

"I've been here all along, so I'm the proverbial frog in the boiling pot—I can't really say what's happened. I wish I understood it."

"Everyone is so indifferent and self-absorbed—don't you agree?"

"Of course," she said.

"How do you stand it?"

"You choose what to pay attention to. I'm lucky. I have my library. Most of my friends are there. And I have my history projects, my ancestry research, and such. It keeps me occupied."

He nodded. He and his mother shared a passion for history. "But how do you ignore the rest?"

"You suck it up, Niall. Stiff upper lip. You're a Bostonian, you should know how to do that."

His brother visited from California. He had a girlfriend, but he'd come alone. His mother took a few days off, and they went to the Cape, stayed in a motel in Wellfleet, walked on the beach and swam until they heard rumors of shark sightings. They didn't discuss anything serious. Liam talked about his job as an assistant district attorney and about his girlfriend Anna who was also studying law. Their mother recounted amusing stories from their childhood, things neither of them remembered. Once they had raided her jewelry box, she said, and set up a table on the street where they laid out her necklaces and earrings to sell. Oh, was she furious! Fortunately, only a single necklace had sold by the time she discovered them. Still, it was worth close to a hundred dollars, and they had sold it for three. They had no recollection of this and, laughing, denied it.

When they returned from that short trip their mother went back to work. Every day Liam made a plan for the two of them— the Museum of Fine Arts, the Museum of Science, the Freedom Trail, the Boston Public Gardens, Faneuil Hall, or the aquarium. They hadn't been to these places since they were young kids, and they remembered little about them, becoming wide-eyed tourists in their own city. But Liam's intent wasn't to see the sights as much as to grill Niall—Niall saw that immediately, saw that had been his mother's intent in inviting him. Every day they replayed the same conversation about Niall's future.

"Aren't you too old to be living off Mom?"

"Sure. I know that. You don't have to tell me."

"Then make a plan, dude. Figure out what's next."

"It's not so easy."

"How hard can it be? It's what everyone does to become a grownup. Mom doesn't like to say this, but she needs her privacy back."

"I'm trying not to intrude."

"You're in the house, man, that's an intrusion."

He knew Liam was right. Liam had always been practical and strategic, governed by rationality and a desire to succeed. He'd never had trouble making decisions as Niall did. Three young girls were stepping onto one of the Swan Boats, their faces agleam with joy, almost beatific. Niall couldn't turn his gaze away, strained to hear their laughter. Oh, to turn back the clock and find such untainted joy.

Liam wanted Niall to make lists of possible professional choices, the pros and cons of each. It was what Liam had done before deciding to become a lawyer. Niall complied—*social worker, librarian, electrician, journalist*—but it was only words on paper, nothing more.

"It's a start," Liam said, perusing the list, "but you have to keep at it. You don't want your life to get smaller and smaller, do you? Are you really considering becoming an electrician? Dad worked all the time and it paid the bills, but I don't think he loved it."

After a week, Liam flew back to California. The visit had left its mark, but still Niall stagnated. He continued wandering, looking around at people and trying to learn how to behave in a fast world while the chants of the brothers remained thick in his ears, trapping him further in the geological speed of his old life.

He was strolling along Mass Ave. from Harvard Square toward

MIT. On a whim, he veered off onto an unfamiliar side street. He followed it for a few blocks and came to a small urban park, play structures on one side, a basketball court on the other. A game was under way, and he paused to watch. The players were teenagers, tall and gangly, two of them white, the others black or mixed race. He marveled at how one minute their loose limbs were far beyond their control, almost flailing, and the next minute the same guy who'd been stumbling would rally his strength, rein in his limbs, and sink the ball, twirling for the rebound on his lean legs with the timing and grace of a ballerina. They bumped each other, hooted, groaned, high-fived, each one a little factory of sound and movement, effusing enthusiasm at being alive. They functioned together like a self-contained system you might study in physics class, moving in and around each other, dribbling and jumping and shooting in response to laws unique to their own bodies. Though the competition was fierce, even personal, they clearly liked each other. They didn't appear to be interested in keeping score, only in flexing their muscles, enjoying what they could do together, and displaying their fit, capable bodies for passersby like Niall. It was almost like theater. One of them flashed a grin in his direction and he grinned back. A few younger boys had gathered on the sidelines to watch along with Niall. They inched forward until they were right at the edge of the action, enthralled and hankering for an invitation to join.

He watched for close to an hour before continuing on his walk, taking the players with him in his head. They were so young and so gifted. But what impressed him most was their instinct for collaboration. When the ball went out of bounds one of them went to retrieve it immediately, without discussion or argument. When a free throw was in order, they all fell quickly into line. He could not discern any hierarchy among them, nor racial tension. And despite their occasional sharp hollering, there was pure joy on that court. He guessed they were fifteen or sixteen; high school students on summer break.

When he left them, he walked back to the T more quickly than usual, and a plan came to him as he went. It was the first idea that had interested him, even excited him. He would teach boys like this. Maybe girls too. While he imparted what he knew about history, they would show him the path back to purpose and joy.

He was hired in late spring, just as he was finishing his teaching certification program. The New Jersey school was thrilled to have him: a former monk with a knowledge of history. He would have so much to offer their population of adolescents who'd had rough beginnings and limited exposure to the life of the mind. They needed guidance and role models, people like him. He was given a tour of the school by the new principal, Dr. Johnson, a white-haired man who came from the world of private schools and had been given the mandate to raise the school's standards, "giving these kids a chance." The locker-lined corridors smelled of DNA from the last century. The concrete walls had been recently painted a pale orange which didn't entirely conceal the graffiti beneath. There was nothing discernibly wrong with the classroom he was assigned to—number thirty-three, the last room at the end of a long hallway—except for a kind of sadness that leaked from the blank blackboard, a twentieth-century relic, and the empty walls. It wasn't a place you would choose to spend time.

"Bit by bit we're giving the whole school a new look," said Dr. Johnson. He reported he was raising funds from private sources across the Tri-State area. The allocated public funds were "ridiculously inadequate." He sounded more like a college president than a high school principal as he described his hopes for a new arts program, a vocational training center, along with many more teachers. Still, Niall liked his ambition and his direct gaze.

As Niall was leaving, Dr. Johnson put an avuncular hand on his shoulder. "You know, I made an exception in hiring you. I was expected to hire a more 'diverse' faculty, not garden-variety white men like yourself, but I decided your status as a former monk offered an important kind of diversity. The diversity of divinity." He laughed. "Prove me right, okay?"

Niall liked that Johnson could joke about his background as a monk. Most people didn't dare mention it, curious but cowed. Maybe they assumed he was a religious fanatic, or that he was passing judgments. Maybe the choice simply branded him as far outside the norm.

6

The faculty members are assigned to rotating lunch supervision which involves two of them at a time circulating among the tables to tamp down rowdy behavior and suppress any conflicts that look as if they're getting too serious. Policing the students this way is not a job any of the faculty members have been trained for and no one likes it, but for Niall especially, it raises dread of a high order. He can barely control the students in his own classroom and can't imagine supervising hundreds of students sprung from class who are eating and socializing, playing music and singing and shouting and tossing whatever they happen to be holding, whether it's meatballs or books. Every week since Niall arrived at the school, there has been some report about an escalating skirmish in the lunchroom that had to be quelled. Wanting to understand what he'd have to contend with, he has peered in and seen the way the students segregate themselves, black and white and brown all at different tables. With a few exceptions even the girls and boys seem to congregate separately. He thinks back to the joyful, collaborative teenagers at the Cambridge basketball court who inspired him to become a teacher and wonders why that spirit isn't more present here. Sometimes the quarrels erupt at a single table, but they often spill between tables too. It doesn't help that the tables are jammed so close together that accidental elbowing is easy.

His first assignment here is with the art teacher Patsy who, with her sing-song voice and gentle manner, appears to be as much of a pushover as he is. But, having taught at the school for over a decade, she doesn't seem daunted. "Just joke with them and it's fine," she tells him, spotting his nerves. He's not a joker, and joking doesn't seem like her strong suit either.

They begin on opposite sides of the room and she dives in, strolling among the tables and touching the shoulders of some of the students, pausing to chat with others, making her presence known. His touch on anyone's shoulder is bound to be regarded differently from hers—the faculty was well-instructed about the ins-and-outs of harassment before school began—but a gentle woman like her can get away with it.

He takes a tentative step between the rows of rectangular tables, absorbing the room's jumpiness in his own body. He searches for students he knows, sees Brittany and Angelina, two white girls from his first period class of freshmen. "Hey there," he says, but they don't hear him, so he moves on, past a table of Puerto Rican and Central American students, wishing Lluvia were here to signal his acceptability by greeting them in Spanish. Next is a table of black boys, then one of girls, some wearing head scarves. No one can fault the school on diversity, but the segregation bothers him. Not surprising, given what he's seen in his own classroom. Still, it's part of the school's mission to encourage the students not only to accept students who are different from themselves, but to come to know them too. "I had a white friend my senior year," Tiffany told him. "But she dropped me when I got into Princeton and she didn't. No big loss there—she thought I only got in because I'm black. That's the kind of friend I can do without." She swatted him, her face in a disingenuous grin. "Anyway, most people aren't as enlightened as you and me, right?"

The students seem more interested in talking than eating and, with all of them vying for attention and all their phones playing

competing music, the volume is ear-splitting. No one pays attention to him. Despite the noise he doesn't see any violation of the
behavior code. No bullying. No fighting. No throwing of food.

A scream from the far side of the room turns everyone's head.
Patsy is standing over a white girl, gesturing to the door. The girl
grimaces and rolls her eyes at her circle of friends, but she obeys,
rising and making her way to the cafeteria exit amidst a hail of
shouts, Patsy following. They vanish into the corridor that leads
to the lobby, leaving Niall alone. He freezes—he can't possibly
monitor the whole room by himself.

"Yo, Mr. O! Want a slice?" It's Jayden, a few tables away, holding
a pizza slice aloft. "Go on, take it. It's clean."

Niall takes the slice because it seems impolitie not to. "Thanks,
Jayden." He'd like to slide onto the bench beside Jayden, but Jayden
is already back in the jig-jagging conversation of his cohort, and
Niall has a job to do. He moves on, holding the limp slice that
leaks grease onto his hand, his shirt, his pants.

"Dude, you're a mess," says a black girl he doesn't know. She
hands him a napkin.

"Thank you," he says, wrapping the slice in the napkin. "You get
an A." It's a stupid thing to say since she's not a student of his, but
he wants to give her something, and grades are the only currency
he holds here, though not a very valuable currency. He vows to
remember her and looks around for a trash can.

A herd of gazelle-like girls advances to the exit. At the door they
huddle in consultation with each other, chafing to leave, though
they're supposed to stay until the bell. He should be over there,
telling them to stay and chill. They glance over their shoulders
and crack the door then make a run for it before he even begins
to move. By the time he gets to the door, it's too late to summon
them back.

There's a clamor behind him. A tiny string-haired white girl
has dropped her tray, flinging spaghetti and red sauce across the

floor. She stands over it, looking as if she's about to cry. She must be a freshman, but she looks young enough to be in elementary school. He has heard that sometimes the students organize an intentional group tray-drop, but this is clearly an accident. A few girls near her take pity, rescuing her tray. One of the girls hugs her. A black girl, he notes with relief.

Then the bell, followed by the tsunami of students surging to the door, bumping him aside until he's alone. The bell still blares as if it's stuck. His fist still clutches the greasy, balled-up slice.

7

Dominic, wearing a T-shirt that reads *Wops Rock*, paces across the designated performing area at the front of the classroom, shimmying his shoulders and stroking the microphone like a veteran rock star. His phone blares a cacophonous song as he marks the beat with his head, bringing his mouth inches from the mic so his outgoing breath can be heard above the music.

Niall, sitting in a chair behind all the tables, still grease-covered, is acutely aware of having set something in motion.

Dominic silences his phone. "My words are: *Great, Nation,* and *Brave.* So here goes . . .

> *There's no debate, this nation's great. iPhones, TikTok, Grand Theft Auto. Superbowl and Jay-Z . . .*
> *So what's your problem, don't tear your hair out, stop going crazee, look around and see,*
> *Don't criticize, antagonize, terrorize,*
> *just recognize, how great we are, will always be.*

Dominic pauses for a few silent beats, scanning the classroom and marking the beat with his head, making sure everyone is paying attention—they are—before he resumes.

Got to galvanize, be one brave country.

Russia can bomb us to smithereens, blow us to a pile of beans, ruin all our dreams,

You wanna die that way, come to stalemate, deteriorate, a very bad fate?

So step up, be strong, don't say we're wrong,

We got our song, get out your bong and sing along,

Let freedom ring.

Everyone claps, acknowledging Dominic's bravery for having gone first. Dominic eyes Niall, waiting for him to respond. Niall hesitates. He shouldn't have trusted himself to wing it. No experienced teacher would have arrived without a more detailed plan. He rises and makes his way to the board where he writes: *War. Polarization. Freedom.* "Are these the themes you were trying to address, Dominic?"

"Yeah. Sure."

"Anyone want to add anything?" No one responds. "Okay, nice job, Dominic. Who wants to go next?"

Several hands shoot up—the usual suspects, Jayden, Rania, Camilla. He'd like to begin with some of the shyer ones.

"Tiffany, let's hear from you."

She lowers her head to the table so her tawny hair covers her face. He can't tell if she's feigning shyness or not. She's a white girl, a follower who hasn't clarified herself to him so far. It's girls like her who used to make him weak with desire, though he never made headway with them, and now he can't see why he liked them in the first place. She comes to the front of the room, sinking her weight into one hip.

"Taylor Swift," she says. She plays a few bars of a song on her phone without mentioning its title. "I can't sing, so here goes. Oh, my words are: *Dead. Devotion. God.*

> *Look at me again.*
> *Turn your head and see—I'm the girl who loves you*
> *Open your eyes, see that I'm your prize.*
> *Don't act as if I'm dead.*
> *You loved when I gave head.*

She pauses and looks up from her sheet of paper with a coy smile. A few of the girls titter. Should he stop her? But she's already moving on.

"Okay, here's the chorus:

> *Just look at me and see.*
> *Forever you and me*
> *You're deep within my heart*
> *We'll never be apart*
> *Just look at me and see*
> *You're a god to me.*

She looks up again, smirking a bit, then resumes, louder now, more confident.

> *You're my devotion*
> *My love is big as the ocean*
> *Can't you see she's a ho', an easy lay*
> *She won't love you all the way*
> *She'll dump you at the break of day*
> *She don't care about your heartache.*

"Okay, chorus again:

> *Just look at me and see*
> *Forever you and me*
> *You're deep within my heart*

> *We'll never be apart*
> *Just look at me and see*
> *You're a god to me.*

"Okay, that's it." She glances at him with more than a touch of defiance, the first real sign of her personality he's seen.

"Thank you, Tiffany." He feels a blush coming on and goes to the board, turning his back for cover. He writes: *Love. Heartbreak.* Of course they're preoccupied with these matters—why would he have thought otherwise? He doesn't write *sex,* hoping it won't come up again so directly. He returns to his seat at the back and presses on. "Okay, next."

No one actually sings their songs, but they recite them rhythmically, stressing the rhymes. Several girls have written songs like Tiffany's about unrequited or lost love, to the music of Beyoncé or Taylor Swift, names that barely register with Niall. The boys write about kicking ass or winning something. They haven't abided by Niall's no-profanity rule, but he doesn't have the heart or the expertise to call them out mid-performance. All their idols use profanity routinely.

Rania, always energetic, is especially pumped today. She wears a dark crimson headscarf and accepts the mic lovingly, cradling it near her chest while she plays a short clip from someone she calls "Cardi B." Most of the words are incomprehensible, but *fuck* and *cunt* are unmistakable. What a fool he was for suggesting this—he wonders what the parents would think if they were here, Rania's Muslim parents in particular. He is in way over his head.

"*Of. By. For,*" Rania says. "Those are my words. *Of* the people. *By* the people. *For* the people. Those are the most important ones, right?"

Niall nods encouragement though Rania doesn't need it. Her phone becomes a metronome, punching out a loud beat she follows

with her hand, up and down, as if she's conducting a marching
band.

> *Say I'm a rag head*
> *They'd rather see me dead*
> *Get out of here, don't ever wed.*

> ***Of, by, for***—*it's not like that, never was like that, never like that,*
> *If you're not like them you must be a rat*
> *Head scarf makes you barf*
> *All you see is trash*
> *Someone else to mash.*

A few of the white boys roll their eyes but, riveted, no one says a
word.

> *See me, Muslim bitch,*
> *I must be a witch*
> *I give lots of sass, won't give you no pass,*
> *Cause I'm a smart ass.*

> ***Of, by, for***—*it's not like that, never was like that, never like that,*
> *If you're not like them you must be a rat*
> *Head scarf—I see you barf*
> *You think I'm brown-skin trash*
> *Someone else to mash.*

> ***Of, by, for***—*it's not like that, get over it,*
> *Cause we're deep in shit.*

"Okay, there you go," Rania says, all business, dipping her head
and returning to her seat. "And by the way, it's not really done yet.
I'm still working on it." Defiant, like Tiffany, defining herself.

Niall nods, afraid to speak into the fraught silence. He slinks to the board. *Racism, Prejudice, Islamophobia,* he writes. *Keep moving, Niall.* Jayden is next.

"I been listening to Ye. Not because I like him as a person, cuz I don't. He's an asshole—pardon my French. But his music is good. My words are: *People. Perish. Prosper.*" He moonwalks back and forth a few times across the performing area as some lines from a song play. "This here is called 'Power.'" He stops the music. "In case you're wondering, I'm lit as shit. Okay?"

> *Studying history*
> *But it's no mystery*
> *It's pretty shifty*
> *This ain't no Gettysburg*
> *Whole thing's absurd.*

He starts the music again and moonwalks for a few more lines before cutting it. The students clap, but he hushes them with a tamping palm.

> *Fuck your boo*
> *Kiss your mother*
> *Only rule is*
> *Love each other.*

This time he moonwalks to silence, letting the words resonate. The students, captured in his thrall, hold to their silence too.

> *In those bad old days*
> *Some hoped for better ways*
> *But we don't see it here*
> *World's full of fear*
> *Shitty atmosphere*

> *Small kids perish*
> *So, say, what do you cherish?*

More moonwalking in silence. A lone call from one of the other boys. "Go, Jayden."

> *Fuck your boo*
> *Kiss your mother*
> *Only rule is*
> *Love each other.*

When he moonwalks this time a few of the other guys join him, then linger behind like a backup band.

> *Ruled by white men ghouls*
> *They be proper fools*
> *Won't no-how get down with their rules.*

He stands still and when he resumes the backup boys speak the lines along with him as if they've rehearsed.

> *Fuck your boo*
> *Kiss your mother*
> *Only rule is*
> *Love each other.*

Niall is speechless. Profanity notwithstanding, they're getting to the heart of the issues he's hoped to discuss, as well as turning in impressive performances. Two students have yet to go: Colton and one of his pals, Mason. Mason claims to have only two lines.

"Well, go up there and share them."

Mason is a skinny squirmy guy with eyes as hyperactive as hummingbirds. He refuses the mic. "It's only one line," he says.

"I don't need a mic. Here goes: *Our teacher was a monk / Now he teaches us pure junk.*" He grins out at the other students, avoiding Niall's look. The other students don't respond.

"Sit down, Mason. And come see me after class. Colton, your turn." Niall's cells will not cohere. How does Mason know he was a monk? It's not something he's told any of his students. He swirls through time, memories surging into the present, the present receding into memory. He straddles parallel dimensions and struggles to press on. He can't afford to freeze. Not now.

"Colton?"

"I don't have squat."

"Well, show us whatever you have."

"Like I said—I've got nothing. Nada." Colton holds up his palms, fingers spread. Niall stares at them, thinking ruefully of Merton's urgings. *It is necessary we find the silence of God not only in ourselves, but also in one another.* It seems impossible that he could ever regard anything about Colton as holy. He commands his swerving body back to the present and is relieved to realize time has run out. Class is over. They'll have to delay the discussion.

"Okay, I'll see you after class too, Colton. Now let's give everyone else a hand. Terrific work. Leave your songs with me. Thank you all."

As the other students swarm his desk, Mason and Colton try to slip out of the classroom unnoticed, but Niall summons them back. The two boys saunter to his desk, unfazed as uniformed cops. Niall is suddenly aware of the huge grease spot on his pants and tries to cover it with his palm.

"Why is it that you both think you don't have to do the work?"

"It's bullshit," Colton says. "It's busywork."

"It may be busywork, but it's busywork with a purpose."

"What purpose?" Colton shakes his head. "If there's a purpose you should tell us what it is."

"You heard the songs—they were addressing serious issues."

"Politics. Pure politics. You're not supposed to bring politics into the classroom, in case you haven't heard."

"You two can write your songs after school in detention today. And Mason—start again—this isn't an assignment about me."

"You said we could write about anything."

"Use your common sense," Niall says. "And use your three words."

"I think you're picking on us," Colton says. "Because we're white."

"I'm not picking on you, but if I were, it would be because you're not doing the work."

"Yeah, right. Like I said—you're picking on us."

As Niall thinks about how to defend himself, the boys are already slipping out the door.

8

They lived in adjacent chambers on three sides of a courtyard. The rooms were Spartan but cozy. A single bed. A small desk. Two lamps. A low bookcase. Hooks for hanging towels. The dark oak walls glowed warm in the lamplight. The single window looked out to the pastures where cows grazed, flocks of birds swooped by, and the seasons crept in to change things. They shared communal bathrooms at each of the building's corners. The doors of the rooms had no locks, a matter of principle in a community where trust and mutual respect prevailed. It made Niall realize how accustomed he'd become to the territoriality of *yours* and *mine*. It took some time to get used to the openness. He had little of monetary value, though there were a few things his mother had given him that held sentimental value: an analog watch with a large face and a soft leather band; several volumes of poetry, one in particular an anthology called *The Solace of Poetry*, inscribed by his mother; and a framed picture of her. Beyond that, he had only the civilian clothes he'd arrived in, his puffy red winter jacket, his toiletries, his journal. He had left his history books behind. He was not here to study history, though living in this building that was over one hundred and fifty years old was like stepping back in time. It was redolent of all the devoted men who had prayed and worked and died here, flecks of their skin and strands of hair lodged in the cracks of the floorboards, preserved over the years like honed fossils, an alchemy that sent up a unique smell that was impossible to describe or recreate.

At night, doors opened and closed. Slippered footsteps traveled the hallways like wind as the men went to relieve themselves. A human hive. It was the communal activities that made Niall's heart soar and invigorated his commitment to knowing God in the deep way his peers did. At the services in the chapel where they sang and chanted and listened to readings, sitting or standing side by side, the boundaries of their bodies seemed to melt so they merged into a single entity, devoted to the same mission. He saw them as a flock of birds or a school of fish. Or perhaps like the cells in the human body, behaving better as a group than they would alone. Emergence. He loved the meals too, the refined choreography of serving and clearing a meal—it always unspooled smoothly, the eating in silence, only the *tap* and *tink* of utensils and bowls as the brothers did what was necessary to nourish themselves. It was all so unexpectedly simple as nothing had been before.

Niall passed the month of his Observership in a dream-like infatuation with his new life, its rituals, its simplicity, its humility, its devotion to something other than self. He had high hopes for communing with God and soothing his erratic temper. Becoming part of the herd of brothers, he was happier than he'd been in years. He missed his mother, but that was a pleasant ache that reminded him of the love they'd always shared.

He was the youngest of the men by far. Most of the others were in their sixties and seventies, three were well into their eighties. Two, the stutterer Brother Martin, and dark-bearded Brother Thomas, were in their fifties, closest in age to Niall though still much older. Most of them traversed the walkways and grounds as if traveling through viscous air, and when they raised their arms to perform various tasks, it looked as if they were performing Tai Chi. Once, late for chapel, Niall was running along the walkway and, as he merged with the others, a voice reached him from somewhere at the front of the pack. "Slow down, Brother. God waits." The words were not harsh, but the voice was harsh. Niall could not see who had spoken those words, but he took their asperity into his flesh as if he'd been physically pierced, hearing the anonymous voice in his head as he tried to sleep that night, wondering why that man had sounded so angry here in the house of God.

He made an effort to slow down, imagining sand bags attached to his limbs, telling himself his arms were made of lead, but he often forgot and worried his lapses into speed offended them.

As the month of Observership neared its end, his postulancy on the horizon, he brought up the question of his youth with Abbot Jerome, with whom he had weekly meetings. He was twenty-seven. "I'm so much younger than everyone else," he said.

"Yes?"

"It's sometimes awkward."

"Life is sometimes awkward, yes."

"I feel as if I'm offending people when I move too fast."

"Does that make you feel superior?"

"No. No." But was he telling the truth? Was he secretly reveling in his body's youthful capabilities?

"God pays no attention to age and nor should we."

"But some of the other brothers seem to resent me."

"If so, that is for them to work out. You and the others are more alike than you are different. Humility helps us to see our similarities. And as time passes you will slow down, and in slowing down, you will be able to hear and know God more keenly."

He loved his weekly meetings with Abbot Jerome, who had a soul that lofted lightly over everything. The Abbot's fallback reaction to the concerns Niall talked about was understanding and forgiveness. The meetings were weekly, and the Abbot asked Niall how he was adjusting, what difficulties he was having with his devotions. He recommended biblical and Cistercian texts he thought Niall might benefit from. He was a teacher by nature, gentle in his direction, always patient. He often seemed amused by Niall.

They met in the Abbot's spacious office with a small babbling water feature. Behind the Abbot's head was a painting of Saint Benedict, their founder, bald and white-bearded, gazing sideways in beatific humility, similar to the Abbot himself. A picture window that took up the better part of one wall looked out on the fields of grazing cows who also looked humble and beatific, needing nothing but the grass before them.

But the solitary hours were always a challenge. There was an obscene amount of time to think, to live inside himself as he read the few lines of text he was supposed to be studying, the goal amorphous. *Lectio Divina: Read. Meditate. Pray. Contemplate.* He was not accustomed to parsing texts so slowly, lingering over each phrase and word as the Abbot instructed him to do. In graduate school he had had so much to read he often skimmed. And this wasn't the same as taking time to savor poetry whose lines and words washed over him as these texts did not. Even the thought of God, who he was trying hard to know, receded from him in this practice, becoming abstract and purely intellectual, not the least bit corporeal as he thought a knowledge of God should be. The quiet expanded his brain into an enormous labyrinth full of choices that led to dead ends. Some days he went through the motions, trusting a close reading of the texts would reveal something true; other days he was desperate for distraction, and he left his chamber when he wasn't supposed to and visited the library or the garden to check on the growth of the peas and beans he had planted, or he watched the chickens pecking in the grass, or if it was winter and snowy, he allowed himself to make a snowball as if he was still a kid. At night he read himself to sleep, treating himself to poetry, a taste of the world he'd left behind.

What different struggles he had faced in that world from those he faced now.

Often, when he was in the garden avoiding study, he ran into the same man, Brother Francis, a cheerful man in his sixties. Francis always greeted Niall warmly. "Trouble with so much studying?" he said the first time they ran into each other. "Why don't we take a walk?" They followed the dirt path, already succumbing to spring mud, which circumnavigated the entire hundred acres belonging to the monastery.

"Hard sitting still?" Francis said.

Niall, still in his postulancy then and not yet given the name Anselm, sighed. "*Lectio divina*—I can't get the hang of it."

"I was that way too. Maybe I still am a bit." He laughed and handed Niall a mini peanut butter cup which Niall took and ate, enjoying the subversive chocolate melting over his tongue.

Over the course of the next several walks—which first took place randomly, then happened weekly, and eventually every couple of days—he learned that Francis had been a stand-up comedian before he joined the monastery. He had achieved a modicum of success, but never overcame his stage fright which caused a crippling pain that roved from one body part to another. He mimed these maladies, clutching his belly, feigning a limp. "I was a mess," he said, laughing.

Niall could see the mischief and buffoonery that had made Francis a comedian, and when he was having difficulty attending to prayer or study, he took heart from thoughts of Francis and his comedic touch.

This other man was Brother Thomas. His dark beard. His blue, unblinking eyes. His surly mien. Niall found him lurking behind corners. Watching. Judging.

He stood in the garden, leaning on his hoe, arresting Niall with his gaze. "What is our highest purpose, Niall?"

Niall stared down at the hillocks of soil they'd been overturning, thought blocked by the suddenness of the question and the attitude effusing from Thomas's dense body. He shook his head. "I'll think about that. Thank you for asking, Brother Thomas."

In the kitchen, Niall couldn't locate the knife designated for cutting the cheese curds.

"What are your thoughts on the Afterlife?" Brother Thomas asked from his perch at the stove.

Please, no, not now. I can't find the knife. Niall hung his head. Thomas handed him the knife.

Niall understood these interrogations as a form of hazing. Perhaps everyone new was subjected to them. But at some point, shouldn't they stop?

Niall was approaching the door to the refectory for the midday meal when Thomas's voice lassoed him. "What do you think of beauty, Niall? Is it good?"

They stepped off the path to let the other brothers pass.

"Well, yes, I think so. God gives us beauty, doesn't he?"

"You don't think it can mislead us?"

"Well yes, I suppose. Sometimes."

Niall would have liked to have those conversations, but they deserved time and thought and should not have been conducted in the midst of other activities when Brother Thomas seemed to want brief, headline-style answers, making Niall feel like a dullard, stumped and ashamed. He tried to imagine how the other brothers might respond to such questions.

When they were assigned to the same work detail—not infrequent—Thomas eyed Niall's work, making sure it was adequate. More often than not, he was present when Francis and Niall returned from their walks, scraping the mud from their shoes with sticks. Thomas shook his head with disapproval as if he had some authority the other monks didn't have.

But—he could be kind too. Apparently, he was aware of Niall's love of poetry, and he left a collection of Neruda poems at Niall's door with a note: *You might like these. BT.* Another time he left a soft facecloth and a pumice stone, as if to say he was sorry for being such a prick. Niall knew he must forgive.

9

He has taken to staying in his classroom long past the official end of the school day, unless he has made a specific plan to meet Trinity. He organizes materials and lesson plans, delaying his departure mostly to avoid the awkwardness of running into anyone, either faculty or students, and having to make small talk. The autumn light fades quickly these days; a muted swath of orange seeps through his west-facing windows, urging him to go home. He wanders among the tables and chairs, picking up debris the students have left: fast food wrappers, hoodies, pencils and pens, and once, a pack of unopened condoms that must have fallen from a pocket. He examines these things as if they're windows into his students' lives, but the objects hold back, retentive. He thought it would be easier to get to know the students, but they turned out to be opaque. He has no idea how they spend their free time, what they want for themselves. Glimmers into these things sometimes emerge in a discussion—references to the jobs they hold down or the video games they play—but not enough to give him any complete picture. How can he teach people he doesn't know? But in his five classes, he has over one hundred and fifty students, far too many to know personally, especially since he isn't an aggressive socializer to begin with.

When dusk takes over and silence has descended in the hallways, he gathers the stack of papers from students, the songs from fifth period on top, and embarks on the long walk down the dim corridor, through the lobby, and out to the parking lot, where his car is usually parked in the corner. Sometimes he detours to the faculty room to collect his mail, scanning the names on the other boxes, trying to attach faces to names. He came to this school imagining he would collaborate with the other faculty members, all of them dedicated to achieving the same ends. He hadn't thought about how balkanized they would all be, confined for most of the day to their own classrooms. If he were to initiate collaboration, he would have to know who they were first.

Sometimes he makes it to his car without encountering another human being, but sometimes there's another teacher who has been working late, or a student—who he might or might not know—leaving detention, or Dr. Johnson, or the janitor Pete just going on duty. Pete is easy to chat with about weather or traffic, but encounters with the others are delicate negotiations. Dr. Johnson inquires about how he's settling in, which necessitates a few minutes of lying and platitudes. The detention students regard him as a confirmed enemy who is likely to punish them. The interactions with other faculty members are hampered by him never knowing exactly who they are, and they don't seem to know him either, so they reintroduce themselves, talk about getting together for coffee, and extricate themselves as quickly as possible.

All his life he's been scooting away from people like this, people he hasn't wanted to talk to or even see. It's no way to live, such constant avoidance, but he has no idea how to go about changing this persisting aspect of himself.

Just as he is about to reach his car, he hears footsteps behind him. He startles and turns to see Mateo, the gentle Latino boy, one of the few students who doesn't scare him.

"Sorry, I didn't mean to surprise you, Mr. O'Malley."

"No worries. I was just lost in thought, you know? You're leaving school late."

"I had tutoring."

"How are you getting home?"

"Walking."

"But it's almost dark."

"I always walk on tutoring days."

"Would you like a ride? It's no problem."

Mateo hesitates, as if reviewing parental warnings. "Well—"

"Come on, get in."

Mateo gets in uttering a stream of thanks, and Niall drives through the dark streets with a surge of elation and confidence despite knowing it is unprofessional to give a student a ride. He likes doing this small, good deed. It makes him feel unexpectedly powerful. He has something to offer Mateo, albeit only a ride.

"How's the tutoring going?"

"Good. She's helping me write sentences the right way. She says I'm getting better."

"That's great. Knowing how to write good sentences will serve you for life, no matter what you end up doing."

"She's going to help with my song too."

"That's good. You got a good start. What did you think of class today?"

"Awesome. Jayden, wow, his song rocks. He's so smart. I could never write a song like that."

"Keep at it, and I'm sure you can. Everyone did a good job."

"Right here on Elm. Number 1270."

"You live on Elm? We're practically neighbors. I live only two blocks away. It's a long walk from here to school. Let me know if you ever need a ride again."

"Thanks, Mr. O'Malley."

Mateo gets out of the car, unleashing more thanks, and Niall watches him walk up to an apartment complex similar to Niall's own. The boy turns to wave before he goes inside. Niall has no idea what awaits him in there. He wonders if other students of his live as close as Mateo does. The thought brings a prickle of claustrophobia. He hasn't given any thought to where his other students live before. Having Mateo nearby is one thing, but there are plenty of other students he'd rather not run into.

He lugs his bags and books up the stairs to his second-floor apartment, turns on some lights, and drops his things. He wishes the place felt more like home, but he focused so much on getting his classroom ready that he ignored his apartment. Every night he surveys it, wondering what would make it more homey. When Lluvia first saw it, she said it looked like the cave of a depressive. They both laughed. He's been depressed on and off, but he wouldn't say he's a depressive. Since then, he's made a few improvements: new bedding—red sheets which Lluvia loves—and some Van Gogh and Matisse prints on the walls. Lots of happy colors. But the living room and kitchen area have not been touched. They're furnished with a few Goodwill items he scored last June. A couch. An easy chair. A desk. All are purely functional and have seen better days. Some color here, too, would be an improvement. He'll invite Lluvia on a shopping trip to help him with choices. Five years of a structured life, in which he made few choices, have left him bereft of a skill that was never his strong suit to begin with.

He declined dinner at Lluvia's tonight. He's been avoiding the topic of moving in with her and Rocio and Flora, not to mention the subject of marriage—he can't wrap his mind around such a big change—but he also begged off because he needs to think about what happened in his class today. Their performances surprised and humbled him, and has no idea what his next move should be. His students are so much smarter and more aware than anyone gives them credit for. Even he, especially he, has underestimated them. He wishes he could get them to perform their finished songs for the whole school, but he knows that it's out of the question with all the sex and profanity they contain.

He lays the pages out before him. Rania's is neatly printed from a computer: "*Head scarf makes you barf / All you see is trash / Someone else to mash.*" Who can dispute this? Jayden's song is scrawled on a piece of yellow lined paper in nearly illegible longhand. But his words are also indisputable: "*World's still full of fear / Shitty atmosphere / When small kids perish / Say, what do you cherish?*" His refrain almost sounds like it comes from the pulpit, if you were to excise the profanity. "*Fuck your boo / Kiss your mother / Only rule is / Love each other.*" Niall has no idea what *boo* means, but he figures it must mean woman or girlfriend. Maybe Trinity would know for sure. Even Mateo, with his two stanzas, had made a credible stab at the assignment. "*I am waiting waiting waiting for my life to start / So many guys around me act as if they have no heart. / I don't talk to no one and no one talks to me / So I hang alone or with my family.*"

The textbook knowledge Niall has to teach them about American history, important as he has always seen it to be, seems almost trivial next to the life experience his students bring to the table. He should have realized this would be the case. How can he bridge the gap between the history he knows and wants to impart to them, and the lives they live daily, the gap between his life experience and theirs? He envies the math and science teachers whose subject matter is so much more straightforward.

He is especially stymied by the intimate love songs many of the girls wrote about vulnerability and heartbreak, about their eagerness to please their men and to have sex if that is what's called for—how can he possibly address these concerns when he is so far from that phase himself? The gender divide between him and them feels like an almost unbridgeable chasm.

Then there's the problem of Colton and some of his allies openly deriding him, undermining everything he tries to do. So far, their negativity has been mostly contained and hasn't affected the other students—he's grateful for that. But he has no idea how to bring them around. They seem so dead-set against him, almost hateful.

Maybe he'll give it some time before he discusses the songs in class. A strategy will come to him in time. Or maybe writing the songs was enough of an exercise, and they don't ever have to have a group discussion. After all, the curriculum awaits; they need to get back to it. Why get entangled in a potentially volatile discussion when it's easy enough to move on?

10

3 a.m. Much too early. Even the birds were not up yet, and the chapel where Niall sat was cold. He restrained a yawn, embarrassed by his continuing failure to be alert at that hour as the other brothers were. He knew he would feel sleep deprived for a while, but he thought he'd adjust more quickly. It was January then; he'd been there since September. The intransigence of the cold didn't help; he was cold even in his puffy red parka that made him stand out, a rude intrusion amidst these white-robed men, but there was nothing to be done about that. He hoped singing would warm him. The black behind the stained glass gave no indication of oncoming light. He breathed deeply, took in the smell of recently applied varnish and stain along with someone's potent fart that rippled back over the pews. He thought of Liam's unending catalog of fart jokes—he always had a new one. *What did the silent fart say to the noisy one?* Niall could never remember the punch lines. Brother Thomas, a row ahead, glanced back at him as if accusing him of the smell. There was no way to defend himself. The Abbot's opening words, asking for God's assistance in prayer, were concluding. They all rose to sing Psalm 121. He kept his voice low, still uncertain of the melodies. His memorization skills had been put to the test since he arrived.

"*I lift my eyes unto the hills / From whence cometh my strength / My*

strength cometh from the Lord / Who made Heaven and Earth . . ."
At least this one he knew.

When they sat, Brother Thomas glanced back again. Niall couldn't read the look, the blue eyes changing unpredictably from midnight to cornflower and back again, so one minute he appeared sinister, the next, gentle.

Brother Francis read the Scriptures which kept Niall from nodding off. He focused on Francis's pock-marked red nose, reminiscent of Rudolph, and tried to imagine what Francis was like on stage, cracking jokes before an audience. He was the only brother who read with real expression, served well by his experience performing. The others delivered the Scriptures in deadly monotones. When Francis wasn't reading, Niall had to pinch his thigh or the space between his index finger and thumb to stay awake. He applied pressure until he induced pain, which kept him from fantasizing about being back in bed. When he became a Novitiate, a date fast approaching, he too would have to read the Scriptures occasionally. He would exchange his street clothes for white robes, and at least in appearance he would not be such an obvious outsider.

Francis read the story of the Good Samaritan, a part of Scriptures that was easy to understand. Niall liked the texts that were easily absorbed, and it surprised him that there were many texts from Scripture that befuddled him, when Jesus did and said things that seemed obtuse. Like the story of Jesus cursing the fig tree for not bearing fruit, though it was not the season for fruit; or the story of the man who ran away naked from where Jesus was staying. What did those stories mean? Niall's own moral compass was uncomplicated—at least it was when he arrived there—you love everyone as well as you can, you act with kindness, and you do the best you can for the greatest number of people. You hold your temper. You love God. Maybe if you're a doctor or a mountaineer, you might encounter situations which would require you to choose between who would live and who would die which makes for ethical complexity, but in the sphere of his own life so far, these challenges had not presented themselves.

There was barely a hint of light on the horizon when they left the chapel. Adhering to The Great Silence, which ran from Compline, the last prayers of the night, to Lauds, at 6:30 in the morning, they followed one another through the chill dark, back to the building that housed them and where they peeled off to their own chambers for an hour and a half of additional rest. Niall wondered how many of them actually slept. Francis said his body had grown used to sleeping for brief periods and rising refreshed. He assured Niall that he, too, would grow accustomed to it. But so far Niall had returned from Vigils each morning exhausted, but too restless to sleep.

The astringence of old urine, cow dung, hay. Niall had never entered a barn before. What an urban disaster he was. The cows were restless at that early hour, mooing and stomping, eager to be milked. Each one was in her own stall, their rumps facing him, which made him nervous about being kicked as he made his way to the end of the barn where Brother Thomas awaited him. Niall was here to learn how to milk. It was still dark out—they'd gone there straight from Vigils. There would be no extra sleep before Lauds that day.

Brother Thomas greeted Niall with a nod. The nameplate on the stall said "Buttercup." The cow shivered, so the skin on her back rippled like the movement of wind over grasses. Niall watched warily, wondering if that was normal. Thomas sat on a stool, gesturing for Niall to take the stool beside him. A tin bucket had been set beneath the udder. A larger bucket sat at Thomas's feet. Thomas placed a hand on Buttercup's flank, exhaling quiet reassurances, more breath than speech, hardly a violation of The Great Silence. He plucked a moistened rag from under his scapular and began to clean the udder. How hairy and wrinkled the plumped skin was, not smooth and pink as Niall might have imagined. It was somewhat like his own scrotum, he thought. Done cleaning, Thomas glanced at Niall to make sure he was paying attention. He placed his hand at the top of the teat and locked thumb and forefinger. He began to squeeze with the rest of his hand. A thin spray of milk jetted forth, splattering loudly against the bottom of the metal bucket. Thomas looked back at Niall again, fixing his gaze as he continued squeezing. *Squeeze, squirt. Squeeze, squirt.* A continuous stream of milk was released, and Thomas created a regular mesmerizing rhythm so he didn't need to watch himself. When the bucket was a little over half full, he stopped and emptied it into the larger bucket. Then he rose from his stool, gesturing for Niall to take his place.

I am a worthless workman, inferior to all, St. Benedict said.

When Niall sat, Buttercup took a few sidesteps and kicked the empty bucket which fell with a resounding clang. Niall righted it and looked nervously at Thomas who spread thumb and forefinger, miming the grip again. Niall put his hand in place. The flesh was soft, much softer than his own. He squeezed. Nothing came. He repositioned and squeezed again. A tiny drop of milk leaked out. Buttercup sidestepped again, mooing, impatient to be relieved of her milk. Niall was embarrassed by his incompetence, his sense of being an interloper. Buttercup was a benign presence, but the sheer size and weight of her was intimidating. Thomas had seated himself on the other stool. His breath was loud and labored. He leaned into Niall as if he were about to wrest control. Niall squeezed and squeezed, failing to produce more than a few drops at a time. He started to pull as he'd seen people do in movies.

"Don't pull, squeeze!" Thomas said in a voice that shocked the morning's tranquility and pierced The Great Silence. More quietly, "Never pull."

Niall continued squeezing, but the amount of milk he was able to release was paltry. How could they possibly milk all these cows within a couple of hours, a task that, at the rate he was going, would take all day?

Thomas shoved Niall out of the way with his forearm and resumed the milking himself. "See, like this? You see?"

Niall saw, but seeing didn't necessarily help. He returned to the stool and tried again.

"Slow down, Niall! You young men—why is everything so fast with you?"

That voice—it was the same harsh one that had told him to stop running.

Thomas departed the stall abruptly, going to milk the adjacent cow, leaving Niall alone with Buttercup. When they heard the bells summoning them to Lauds, Niall had filled less than half a pailful, while Thomas had milked three more cows.

Day after day Niall returned to the barn after Vigils, sometimes with another brother, but Thomas was usually there too. They left Niall to himself, but Thomas always checked on him, positioning himself at the end of the stall with that ambiguous gaze of his and that concealing dark beard of his and his heavy breathing. Sometimes he moved close and patted Niall's hand. *Good job.*

Niall was getting the hang of it. Soon he could empty two cows in the time between Vigils and Lauds, and he quickly worked his way up to three or four cows, as many as Thomas was able to do. Though he hated missing the extra hour or so of sleep, he was adjusting to that too. Thomas still checked on him, always finding something to criticize, usually ironically, telling him, breaking The Great Silence, to tell him to slow down. Why should Niall slow down if the milking was getting done and the cows aren't objecting? He touched his shoulder or hand as if he regretted his words.

The end of Niall's postulancy was only two weeks away. He would receive his new name then, one of the two he had submitted to the Abbot, along with white robes. Though he worried about keeping white robes clean, he looked forward to blending in with the others.

It was March, and spring had come early. The warmth and sprouting of greenery excited him, and he and Francis walked more quickly than usual, the squish of mud beneath their shoes a regular soundtrack. Without warning, a leaden cloud arrived and released a delirium of fat flakes that tumbled into the green grass and dandelions. Stricken by the beauty and improbability of the moment, they stopped walking and looked up and laughed. After a minute or so the flakes evaporated. The snow emboldened Niall.

"What is wrong with Brother Thomas? Why is he so mean to me?"

Francis ejected a private chuckle. "My dear boy, pay no attention. Brother Thomas is only responding to your youth. It isn't hatred, only envy, which he has trouble concealing. Your youth among us old folks is truly something to behold. We'd all love to be young again, as you are." Francis's red nose had begun to drip, and he lifted his robe to wipe it.

They moved on, Niall captured by an array of new thoughts. He'd never thought that envy was the explanation for Thomas's odd behavior, although it did explain his objection to Niall's speedy walking. But if that was the problem, what could Niall do to rectify it?

"Being hated isn't comfortable—I sure know that," Francis said. "There were certain times when I was performing and people in the audience abhorred me, and there was absolutely nothing I could do. Once a comedian's performance begins to go south, there's no way of recovering. You're stuck and it gets worse and worse. A terrible, inevitable slide. People would say vile things. Unrepeatable things. Things I would never say to anyone. They acted as if I was a murderer when all I'd done was fail to entertain them. Sometimes they threw things at me: pretzels or half-eaten sandwiches, whatever they had on hand. Once, an apple hit me on the arm and I had a bruise for days. I learned to bail early if things weren't going well. It's only a performance, you think, before complete strangers, so why should their hatred hurt? But it leaves its mark, even anonymous hatred. Some endure it unscathed, but I didn't have the stomach for it. This is all to say, whatever Brother Thomas is thinking, I'm sure he doesn't hate you."

Francis dug into his pocket and withdrew two fun-size Milky Ways, one of which he handed to Niall. "This should soothe your soul." Francis tittered and Niall noticed the sorry state of his teeth. Niall popped the chocolate into his mouth and sucked until it softened and spread over his entire oral cavity, settling around his molars.

"There is, however, something else I think you should know." Francis had lowered his voice, as if someone might overhear them, though they were over a mile from the buildings. "Brother Thomas is the Abbot's nephew. The Abbot brought him here after he got into trouble with the law."

"What kind of trouble?"

"Drugs, I believe. I don't know all the particulars."

"What else *do* you know?

"Very little. And I don't ask because the Abbot made it very clear that he doesn't want us talking about it. That was maybe fifteen years ago when Thomas arrived. I believe that the Abbot knew the judge involved in his case, and they made some kind of deal. You know, to keep Thomas on the straight and narrow. That's really all I know, and some of it is speculation. So no one here says a word about it, and you mustn't either."

"No, no, of course I won't. So you're saying if he weren't here, he would be in jail?"

Francis shook his head. "Maybe."

By the time they got back from their walk the temperature had plummeted and a gray cloud cover had come in. Winter wasn't yet over, despite the greenery. They stopped by the laundry room and used sticks to pry the clods of mud and cow dung from the soles of their shoes. Francis spotted two ticks on his bare ankles. "Early for ticks," he said.

In the kitchen, he found some tweezers from the medical case on the shelf. He plucked the ticks with zeal and dropped them into a dish of alcohol, and the two of them watched the flat brown bodies writhe in death, their skinny legs twitching, both privately wondering if they should be enjoying this sight as much as they did. A few brothers were chopping vegetables, prepping for the evening meal. Thomas was among them. He laid down his knife to consider Niall and Francis. *Stop watching us,* Niall thought. *I don't want you to watch me anymore.* But what could he do? When Thomas smiled at him, he smiled back.

11

"You're a badass," Trinity says, "but I gotta ask—how can you *not* know Cardi B? She's everywhere."

He shrugs. Trinity has a way of making him feel sheepish.

"You can't teach these kids if you don't know the music they listen to. Cardi B is a household name!" She shakes her head. He's a lost cause.

He sighs, defenseless. Of course she's right. They're walking to the parking lot together. It's Friday. The students performed their songs on Tuesday, and he has let the days go by since then without discussing them. Telling Trinity is a confession of helplessness.

"Let me guess—you don't have a TV either?"

Right, no TV. "My girlfriend Lluvia thinks that's a good thing. She's trying to keep her daughter from becoming addicted to screens." It's a relief to have finally worked Lluvia into the conversation. They arrive at Trinity's red Ford Focus. She unlocks it and digs for her phone in her purse then throws her two bags into the car. She turns to him and pokes her forefinger into his chest.

"Okay, it's one thing for her kid, another thing for you. You're not a monk anymore—you're a *high school teacher!* You gotta know certain things! You can't be acting like you wish you'd been born into another century. Plus, with that assignment you gave them, you put yourself smack in the middle of their world. So you gotta follow up. Talk to them about it. You set something in motion—

you can't just ignore it." Outside the school she talks differently to him than when they're in the lunchroom where she keeps her voice low, her gestures restrained.

"I know you're right, but it's not so easy."

"I'm gonna teach you some stuff. Are you on TikTok or Instagram? Spotify? No, of course you're not. Okay, let's start with getting you on Spotify. And YouTube. Get yourself some ear buds and I'll tell you what to listen to. Oh man, I saw some hopeless cases in college, but no one quite as far gone as you!"

She props her phone against the windshield and plays a few seconds of a music video. Her shoulders mark the beat. "That's Bad Bunny. Here's some Pop Smoke." She begins another song, moves to that one too. She's relaxed, showing off her loose joints and relishing his ignorance. "This is Drake." She pauses the music and rips out a sheet of notebook paper to write him a list and thrusts at him.

"Your homework. Listen to these artists, okay. Report back to me next week about the ones you like best."

Drake. Ozuna. Lizzo. Burna Boy. Rosalía. Lil Baby. 21 Savage.

He lingers in bed on Saturday morning, props his phone against a pillow, and watches YouTube videos of Trinity's music. People dance, drink beer and neon cocktails, pilot behemoth vintage cars with headlights flashing. Women in bikinis flaunt the dark cleavage of their sheeny breasts, waggle their voluptuous buttocks within inches of the camera. It's hard to think of these people as artists. He can't look. He can't look away. Many of the lyrics are in Spanish, which he doesn't speak, but even most of the words in English he doesn't understand, obscured as they are by the music's discord. Yet there's no doubt as to what the songs are about. Angst. Rage. Yearning for things to be better. That, at least, he understands. The only legitimate response to the broken world.

He can only watch for a short time. He can't find patterns in the music and the frank near-nudity alarms him, much as he wishes it didn't. He clears his head with Gregorian chants, their simple melodies rendered by a single unaccompanied male voice. This is the music that first lured him into the monastery. There is yearning in this music too, but no rage. Still, he can only listen to chants for so long, as they transport him back to the monastery, and he ends up wedged between the two worlds, wondering where he belongs.

At one o'clock, he and Lluvia meet for burgers at a small, noisy cafe where the tables, within inches of one another, barely have room for their two plates.

"So you do or don't want to live with me—with us? Marry me." she says, grinning, goading, guiding him toward what she believes is his underlying desire.

"It's not that I don't . . . I just need time. Let me think, okay?"

"I get it. You're telling me to back off. You have trouble committing—blah, blah, blah. But if I leave it to you, years could go by and we'd both be geezers. Don't you feel how time goes by and leaves us all in the dust?"

"Not really. I'm not fast wired like you. I'm slow."

"Oh, really? Plus, I'm not getting any younger. If we want a baby, we should get married." A baby? Is she serious?

Though she has been talking more than he, she is already halfway through her burger, while he has taken only two bites of his. A trickle of ketchup, indistinguishable from blood, runs down her chin. Impervious, she continues to eat. Everything about her glows with appetite and zest for forward motion. Has she ever procrastinated? If so, he hasn't seen it. She tears ahead in brazen pursuit of what she wants. No apparent fear of rejection—or perhaps she's simply ready to handle whatever rejection comes. He reaches across the table and dabs her chin with his napkin, surprised by the forwardness and intimacy of his own gesture. "Sorry."

She laughs. "Don't be sorry. If you're wiping my chin you want to live with me. What great old people we'll be!"

On Sunday they walk on the beach with Flora. It's a chilly, breezy autumn day.

With Flora present, they can't discuss the question of living together—Flora's opinions on everything are much too forceful.

"If only my patients would get out here. And get in the water too. It would cure them so fast, I think. They're so darn sedentary."

"Like me?" he says.

"Like you, but worse!" She laughs.

"Hey, Flora, what music do you listen to?" he asks.

She casts him a wary glance. "Ozuna. Taylor Swift. A bunch of people. Why do you want to know?"

"Just curious. Do you know Cardi B?"

"Everyone knows Cardi B."

"What do you think of her?"

Flora eyes Lluvia and shrugs. "She's okay."

"Do you know Cardi B?" he asks Lluvia.

"The name, yes. Not the music, only a little."

"You probably don't need to hear it."

"It's just music," Flora says. "It doesn't mean anything, Mami."

On Monday, Niall, determined to end his procrastination, makes sure to arrive at his fifth period class on time; he's sitting at his desk when the students arrive, less queasy than usual. Some of them look exhausted, because of weekend jobs or too much partying, he surmises.

He has transcribed the words he collected from their performances onto the board again. *Justice. Democracy. Racism. Sexism. Prejudice. Islamophobia. Battles. Bravery. Optimism. Change. Fairness. Love.*

He stands quietly in front of his desk until the students notice him.

"Uh-oh, we're in trouble," Roman says.

Niall laughs, shakes his head, and points to the board. "These are the themes that came through in your songs. Does anyone want to say anything about any of these words or themes?"

The students stare at the board, listless. The weekend has wiped their memories, along with their enthusiasm.

"Come on—it's Monday!" Jayden whines. "We can't think on Monday."

"Your songs were powerful. Doesn't anyone want to comment on what they revealed?"

More contrails of silence.

He tries to imagine what he would say himself if he were a student in the class. He stares at the words and sees, suddenly, how uninspiring they are. They're abstractions, grandiose and boring, the words of platitudes and binary thinking. They're exactly the kind of words that hung him up so often as he pored over texts in the practice of *Lectio Divina*. What did *Devotion* mean? What about *Grace*? Or *God*? Or *Spirit*? For that matter what did *Love* mean? And the word that always confounded him most—*Evil*. So often those words resisted interpretation until they lost meaning altogether, their surfaces glossy, mercurial, refusing to be caught and understood. He sees himself bent over the desk in his chamber, head in his hands, trying to stave off despair.

He remembers how skillful Abbot Jerome was at steering a conversation without making it seem as if he was exerting any force at all, while still maintaining clear authority. He used a light touch—a modest tilt of his head, a raised brow to register disagreement, possibly the slightest grimace or frown. Nothing that would intimidate. His correctives were all stated as questions: Maybe this? Maybe that? He understood how a person recoils instinctively from commands.

"Okay, let's start over. Forget history for a minute. I want you to look at these words and think of a story from your own life that touches on one of the words. A story about bravery, maybe. Or love. Or justice. Tell us a story."

Another seesawing silence. Maybe. Maybe not. He feels like a politician casting about for a constituency.

Dominic lights up. "Hey, Angel, you got a good story. Tell them about your dad."

Angel looks panicked. He's a shy guy, Dominic's sidekick.

"Go on, tell them. It's awesome," Dominic urges, slapping Angel's shoulder.

"Hold on, Dominic. Do you want to tell us, Angel?" Niall prompts.

Angel shrugs, blushes. "My dad—he's a cop—he found a baby in a dumpster at the mall."

Dear God, no, Niall thinks.

"The baby was almost dead," Dominic explains.

"Hush, Dominic. Let Angel tell us." Niall does not want to hear this story. He wonders if he should intercede, change the topic. Angel, too, is not so sure, but everyone is waiting, already firing questions and opinions at him. *That was your dad?!*

"Okay, okay . . . So, like, he did CPR and the baby came back to life. And—"

Aliyah stands, so loud and imperious everyone takes notice; she leaves her seat and strides to Angel. "No WAY!" She thrusts an accusing finger at him. "I *know* that baby. That's my cousin's baby. They wanted to arrest her! She had that baby in the bathroom at the mall and they wanted to arrest her! She only threw it away because she thought it was *dead!* That was your dad?!"

"I don't know," Angel says, clearly wishing he were somewhere else. Aliyah stabs his back with her forefinger. Angel closes his eyes.

"It wasn't her fault. She didn't know. She thought the baby was dead. It was stupid to arrest her."

The class ignites. They've all heard different versions of this story, and they all think their version is the right and true one. It's up to Niall to reset. But how, when he, too, is stuck on images of the baby in the dumpster, the girl in the bathroom giving birth? From the depths of his horror and distaste, he too wants to know more. How Aliyah's cousin managed to give birth alone. How big the baby was. How Angel's father discovered the baby. Where the baby is now. Something outside on the playing field snags his attention. A dog that looks like a fox runs across the grass, then disappears from view. A plastic bag blows in on a gust of wind, then sags like someone dying. Niall has the feeling again that he's in a movie, a New Wave French movie from the twentieth century.

"Shut UP!"

To his amazement, they do. They haven't seen him yell, really yell, quite like this, with such passion and force. "Look, we can go back to the textbook, or we can continue to tell stories. We'll take a vote."

No one wants the textbook. Stories win out.

"Okay. But if we continue with the stories, the rule is: No interrupting or arguing or challenging anyone else's story. Okay? If you don't abide by that rule, we go back to the text."

Energy surges again, and stories begin to cascade from them.

Daniella and her sister were sexually assaulted by her uncle at her *quinceañera*.

Shannel was held at gunpoint on Ocean Beach last summer.

Axel's dad, who almost starved in Afghanistan fighting the Taliban, had to kill and eat a camel.

They are all vying for Queen or King for a day. Niall can almost hear them thinking: *You think that's bad—I've got one for you!* Are these stories true, or are they wildly embellished? He has no way of knowing.

Jordan's dad won fifty thousand dollars for being wrongly imprisoned.

Rania was chased from a Manhattan boutique for wearing a headscarf.

Niall listens, semi-paralyzed, wondering if he should comment, but knowing he wouldn't have any idea what to say. Should he be connecting their stories to the words on the board? Doing so would certainly interfere with the building momentum. He is as engaged by these stories as the students are. Each one cracks open something that makes him want to know more. But he's also mindful of the possibility that Principal Johnson will enter unannounced, asking him why he's ignoring the prescribed curriculum. This *is* American history of sorts, anecdotal history like the work of Studs Terkel, but Niall might have trouble justifying that, even to open-minded Dr. Johnson.

Colton's expression is impassive—still, he's paying close attention.

Mason's father killed a rattlesnake in Arizona last summer.

Anthony's mother was bitten by a rat in the subway.

An unknown person in Gianna's neighborhood is killing all the dogs—no one knows why, but every morning, a few more dead dogs are discovered. Some poisoned. Some shot.

"Doesn't anyone have a happy story?" Niall finally asks.

Everyone laughs. "Happy is boring," Jayden says.

"Yeah," says Rania. "Wasn't there a writer who said something like that? Anyway, like Jayden said, happy *is* boring."

"My younger sister is pregnant?" Roman offers.

"Congratulations," Niall says, even as he computes how young she must be, much too young for motherhood. What is he to make of this? He needs help. He wishes someone else he knows were here as a witness: Lluvia, Trinity, his mother, Abbot Jerome.

The stories continue until the bell rings. Not everyone speaks, but it doesn't matter. What matters is they're listening to one another. Niall has the sudden impulse to run into the hallway and summon the whole school. *Listen to my students. They're talking about the Human Condition. Open your heart.* Maybe God is listening too.

12

His comb was gone. A trivial thing, easily replaceable. His silky light brown hair never stayed where he combed it anyway. Still, it made him crazy to lose track of his things when he had so little to keep track of in the first place. He checked every inch of his small chamber—all the surfaces, the floor, under the bed—and then the bathroom, embarrassing himself when Brother Joseph found him on his hands and knees under the sink, patting the linoleum. *Gremlins*, he said to himself. *Poltergeists*. He considered that spending so much time thinking had reduced the material world to insignificance, causing him to lose track of things. Maybe that was not a bad thing. Eventually, when he had finished his Novitiate and he took his temporary vows, he would have to relinquish his few personal possessions anyway. He wondered how that would feel, giving up the items his mother had given him—the watch, the inscribed poetry book—things he cherished. His attachment to these things was fiercer than he would have liked to admit. But he'd already given up so much—how difficult would it be to get rid of a few more objects? He raked his silky hair with his hands, remembering with amusement how, in the outside world, he sometimes used a hair gel to fix it in place.

He laid on his bed and began the body scan he learned to do in the mindfulness seminar he participated in years earlier with Jon Kabat-Zinn, closing his eyes and beginning at the top, envisioning each body part and trying to relax it: the crown of his head, his skull, his forehead, his face, his neck. He waited for the tension to ease, the silly attachment to his plastic comb to fade. *The Lord is my shepherd I shall not want.* "Stop wanting so much," his mother used to say when he and Liam begged for toys or candy, or any shiny thing that caught their attention. "Wanting is ugly." He had no idea what she meant back then—the things he wanted were far from ugly. LEGO sets and pinball games and gumball dispensers. They were colorful and full of interest—how could you *not* want them? *He leadeth me beside the still waters / He restoreth my soul.* He thought of Francis's unending stash of candy, surely a violation of the monastery's rules, and wondered who else knew about it. But no one would question Brother Francis's deep devotion, so why should it matter? Niall was certainly not going to report him. But the stupid comb—he couldn't help but cycle back to it—wanting it back, valuing that piece of black plastic more than he ever had. He was annoyed at himself for losing it in the first place. Did the other brothers go through such mental gymnastics?

What did it mean to *want* something? Couldn't desire sometimes have the positive effect of moving a person forward to achieving things? How else would you come to know God without fervently *wanting* to know God? It's only a piece of cheap plastic.

A shirt went missing, one of the four shirts (two for summer, two for winter) that he rotated, as he had not yet earned his robes. It was a flannel shirt, soft and green, a layer of protection from the gusts of wind that swooped between the buildings. He had always felt such gladness each time he put that shirt on, felt it soothing and warming his skin.

He checked the laundry, once again crawling on the floor behind the washer and dryer and utility sink. It wasn't there. It was only a shirt, well-worn, but he wanted it back. He mentioned it to the Abbot in his weekly meeting and the Abbot chuckled. "The material world, Niall. It always does us in. When I first joined the order, I was very attached to a car I owned. It was a white Peugeot, secondhand, with a sun roof so I could see the sky as I drove. How glorious it was to drive at night and see the full moon. I bought it with money I'd earned building decks and fences. I even named that car, Flossie. Now I can't believe I was so in love with an engine and a hunk of metal, but back then it was hard to part with her. Another life, shall we say. Now, let's focus.

"*I lift up my eyes unto the hills: from whence cometh my help,*" the Abbot said, half speaking, half singing, enticing Niall to join with a beckoning twinkle in his eyes.

It was 3 a.m., and a single shoe had gone missing. He had only one pair of shoes, not the least bit special—gray athletic shoes a few years old. Rubber soles. Synthetic material on top. They weren't waterproof or mud-proof, but they were comfortable for walking. He needed it to get to Vigils.

He sat on the edge of his bed in the chilly dark, fully dressed but for his shoes. He couldn't think that early, his problem-solving mind not yet activated; the only way he got moving was by force of habit, the urge to return to sleep almost irresistible. After Vigils he was on milking duty. The barn's floor was frigid cement covered with urine and cow excrement no matter how often it was sprayed down. To walk in there and do the milking with the cows' hooves so proximate, shoes were definitely required. Getting himself to the chapel required shoes too. It was only a five-minute walk, but just as they thought spring was coming, a second winter had blown in and the temperatures had been in the twenties, sometimes sinking down to the teens. Recent snowfall had left a fresh eight-inch layer that wasn't melting quickly.

Skipping chapel would draw unwanted attention. He pictured

himself walking there in one shoe, the other foot socked but shoeless. The icy flagstones, the patches of unavoidable snow, the pools of water where someone had thrown down sand. The bells were ringing, traveling with clarity through the still dark morning, summoning them. *Now.* He heard the other brothers leaving their chambers and filling the hallways. There were few other people awake in Western Massachusetts at this hour. Niall usually loved the solitude of early morning.

There was only one thing to do. He put on his single shoe, tied it tight, grabbed his bright red L.L. Bean down jacket, suddenly mobilized. He opened the door to the corridor. Thomas, idling against the wall, turned to face him. "Do you need help, Niall?"

Niall eschewed the offer of an elbow, and proceeded down the hallway. Outside he hopped along, peg-legged, trying to find dry flagstones for his stocking foot. Thomas followed, staying in close range. Niall's socks were quickly soaked. He entered the chapel with Thomas still in his wake and searched for an empty seat. They were late. The Abbot, standing at the dais, stopped his invocation to prayer and nodded to two available seats at the end of a pew up front. Why did the Abbot want them up there? There was plenty of room at the back. Did he wish to humiliate Niall? That was not the Abbot's usual way. *Unhesitating obedience,* says St. Benedict. Niall limped up the aisle, his gait uneven, his sock squishing audibly. Thomas followed like a chaperone. The Abbot resumed speaking.

Sitting on the hard pew in his puffy eye-catching jacket and wet sock, next to Thomas who was dry and neat, he felt dismally out of place. A time traveler from the modern world, the crass, secular world that the others had all renounced. Had they seen he had only one shoe? Some of them must have. He heard them thinking: *How pitiful Niall is, how prone to problems—does he really belong among us?*

13

The covers have slipped from Lluvia's smooth brown shoulder, its curve like an element of the landscape, a distant hill or a sand dune, an enchanting place one would love to inhabit for a long time. Her cheek follows a different kind of curve, her buttocks yet another. A corkscrew of hair dangling across her forehead bobs slightly each time she exhales. He could watch her forever in sleep, meditating on the details of her female body, still disclosing itself to him.

Though he has lusted unrequitedly for many women, Lluvia is only the third woman he's had sex with. The first was at a drunken high school graduation party, when a buxom woman with Raphaelite hair came onto him, a woman whose name he never learned. He was in the kitchen of an unfamiliar apartment where the party was being held, getting himself a beer. He turned from the fridge, beer in hand, already drunk, when this woman appeared before him, radiant and eager, seizing his hips. Without any exchange of words, she slid her hands down the length of his body until she was kneeling on the linoleum, unzipping his trousers and taking him into her mouth. He was too shocked to resist. He remembers leaning his back against the rickety oven handle, staring down at the red line of her part, gripping his sweating, unopened beer, people coming and going. He was so drunk he felt invisible. He ejaculated in a profuse slow-motion arc that landed at the center of the kitchen. His beer bottle dropped and rolled noisily across the floor. He dashed to the bathroom and vomited, and when he emerged, she was gone. The memory still makes him shudder.

The second woman, Amanda, was a brassy, brainy, cheerful woman in his grad school cohort who dominated their class discussions and later earned her PhD as a Medievalist. She too took the initiative with Niall, inviting him for a walk at the Arnold Arboretum where they strolled around the grounds among the majestic trees: magnolias, red maples, oaks, cedars. After that, they got together a few times a week for walks and talks and meals and sex. She was a plump woman who called herself "body-positive" and she kidded him about his inexperience, but she was tender and generous in bed. One morning, after they'd been together for four months and had been spending almost every night together, she emerged from the bathroom (hers) while he was still in bed. "Niall, honey, I think that's it for us. I like you, but I can already see I'm never going to reach you." She sat on the edge of the bed and laid her hand on his blanket-covered knee. "Some part of you is always on Pluto." He had never expected the relationship to last, but still he was taken aback—and hurt—by her honesty.

They spent another year in grad school taking some of the same classes and trying to be cordial with each other. At the end of the year, she invited him out for coffee and told him not to personalize what had happened between them because she realized she'd been a lesbian all along. When he told her he planned to become a monk, she said, "that figures," and he took it as a kind of blessing.

Lluvia is number three.

These nights with Lluvia, sleeping naked, which she insists on doing, skin against skin, breath synchronized as they succumb to sleep, are a kind of ecstasy he never expected to encounter. Until now his moments of ecstasy have been solitary experiences, most often connected to being alone in the natural world. He never knew he could be transported in the presence of another human being, but when Lluvia turns her jigging eyes on him and fixes them there, and he witnesses them slowing from a jig to a tango, he feels himself swooning as if he has finally come to know the entity called God that he spent his years in the monastery trying and failing to know. This connection with Lluvia is so much more than mere sex.

But something disturbs him about the sex. When he is so taken by desire he thrusts himself inside her; she sometimes winces but never objects, and the delight of being there in the velvet interior of this remarkable woman is so intense it is almost painful, and as the seismic waves of sensation alter him, he sometimes forgets who he is and who she is, and afterwards he's sure there's something fundamentally wrong in having gone off by himself, deserting her for his own pleasure.

She has taught him how to bring her to climax, and he likes that he's become proficient at that, but it bothers him that they must travel alone and separately for their pleasure after connecting so profoundly through their eyes. If only they could both achieve climax through simply gazing at one another.

He has been thinking recently about the moment he decided to enter the monastery. He and Amanda had parted by then, and the pressures of graduate school had escalated to an intolerable peak. Reading so much about the Civil War—which he expected to write about in his dissertation—had begun to depress him. So much acrimony. So many people acting badly, with cruel intention. It made him begin dreaming again of monastic life. No one knew that he'd been thinking about this on and off since grade school.

In fifth grade, his music teacher Mrs. Sisson played Gregorian chants for them, explaining the intervals that made it sound peaceful and eerie. Hearing it, his spine tingled and he imagined entering a cave with a book and a mug of warm honeyed milk. She showed them pictures of cloistered monasteries with robed monks reading and praying and singing. "These men have consecrated their lives to God," she said. He didn't know what consecrated meant, but he loved the feeling the chanting gave him—the pictures, too—and he held onto that feeling, and when bad things happened he comforted himself with the certainty he would one day be a monk, hermitted and unassailable.

He had grown up in a Catholic household that paid little attention to God. It occurred to him at some point that none of them—not his father or mother or Liam—really believed in God, though they went to Mass sometimes and took communion and very occasionally went to confession. And they sent him and his brother to parochial school, run by men and women who were staunch believers and who taught them the catechism and expected them to have been baptized. He knew a handful of truly devout people—some of his teachers and parents of his friends— and he understood his family was not that way. So, he kept his thoughts of becoming a monk to himself, knowing they might not approve. His mother in particular would not like it. Once she had said she didn't know why she bothered to go to church when religion felt to her like an elaborate superstition, merely a way to protect yourself from the fear of the nothingness of death.

But it bothered him that he didn't understand God at all, and no one could explain who or what God was despite the fact that so much, like churches and schools, had been organized around the idea. In grade school he could only think of God as a feeling, similar to the feeling he had when he was sick and laid in bed with his eyes closed, and his mother stood over him, her voice low and quiet, her warm body blocking him from harm. He held this idea to himself, because everyone around him referred toGod as "He." If God turned out to be anything like his mother, there was hope that he could begin to understand whatever he or she was.

Sometime in early high school he realized he must be wrong. Everything he heard and read, the Bible itself, embraced a God that was nothing like his mother. This God was the opposite of female. He was judgmental and sometimes cruel, and he did not want you to satisfy yourself with sex or pleasure of any kind. It wasn't a happy realization, and it turned him away from his dream of becoming a monk.

But in grad school, as the stress intensified, the lure of a quiet monastic life returned to him with renewed force. He began reading the work of Thomas Merton, a Cistercian monk whose path to the monastery was known to be circuitous. Merton had been a drinker and womanizer and a man who sought intellectual status, but with time he overcame these vices and became devout. Reading Merton's painfully honest account of his struggles in *Seven Story Mountain,* Niall felt more certainly than ever that he'd been made for that life. Understanding God, he hoped, would follow.

He began attending Mass regularly, trying to pray, which he hadn't done since high school. He achieved a modicum of peace at church, but as soon as he returned to his daily life of classes and exams, the pressure overwhelmed him again. He enrolled in a ten-week mindfulness class run by notable meditation master Jon Kabat-Zinn. Zinn's presence was charismatic, his voice gravelly and hypnotic. In that class Niall began to center himself. He expanded his breathing capacity, learned to scan his body, and made time for daily meditation. He understood that all his life, since he was eight years old and staring into the bathroom mirror, he'd felt the presence of something he couldn't name, and he now realized it must have been God. He initiated conversations with the priest, asking him about his path to the vocation, and he continued to read Merton's writings, thinking of him as a mentor and friend.

"The spiritual life," Merton wrote in *Thoughts on Solitude,* "is first of all a matter of keeping awake." This idea made sense to Niall, and it stuck with him, and he vowed to stay awake. And, as he listened endlessly to Gregorian chant, he began picturing himself as one of the chanters.

One day, when he was prepping for exams that he and his classmates had been dreading, he borrowed his brother's car on a whim and drove out to the Cape, his knuckles blanching from a too-tight grip on the wheel. He had no destination in mind, was driving because it was the only way he could think to escape his worries, though of course they accompanied him the entire way, dutiful chaperones hunkered on his shoulders like gargoyles, determined to oversee whatever he did.

It was a blustery day in early May, one of those days that screams of seasonal change—cumulus clouds with business in mind, not the least bit dreamy, sailing past at a swift clip. At the Cape's elbow the road bent north, the traffic thinned, and the sun was no longer in his eyes. The directional change calmed him, and he relaxed into his body again and realized he was famished, having only had coffee before he set out. In Wellfleet, he stopped at a roadside stand to devour an order of fish and chips. The salt and grease energized him, and a little further on he parked in an empty lot and followed a path that crested the dunes and descended to the beach. After the car's relative silence, the din of the natural world took him by surprise. Wind thrashed his face and whipped the beach grass and stirred up tiny whirlpools of sand. The histrionic gulls squawked at small slights. Squalling terns and cormorants and the meek chirps of the plovers, all vocalized against the background of serious surf. When he descended to the beach, sandpipers sensing his arrival skittered farther down the sand. So much life!

There were ways of seeing all this activity as objectionable commotion, but that day, coming from the rigidity of academia and standing on the wet sand gazing out across the water to where the earth curved toward Europe and the Middle East and Africa, he felt calm. The world was large and full of promise, and he understood he could change his life. He didn't have to slog on to complete his PhD. He could quit and seek a life that, instead of being riddled with anxiety, would be pure and sacred.

As he was contemplating this, a shadow swooped up behind him, darkening the sand, a peregrine falcon flying so low he ducked instinctively. The bird flew out over the water, made a swift dive for a fish, then retreated back down the beach and over the dunes, the doomed dying fish dangling from its beak. Niall stared down the empty beach long after the falcon had disappeared from sight, thinking of the dead fish and the satisfied falcon, life and death feeding on each other, needing each other, and he felt as if he himself embodied everything he'd seen—the shadow, the bird, the fish. He encompassed all of nature's eat-or-be-eaten world within his own body and was overcome by the complexity of this system and the laws that governed it, if there were such laws: the coexistence of nihilism alongside a moral code. He craved to understand coexistence, a force which he now believed was God. History was fascinating and instructive, yes, but it did not reveal much goodness about mankind. Devoting a life to the contemplation of the here and now, the igniting spirit that made the falcon and the fish and his own brain possible—wouldn't that enable him to discover and celebrate, even boost, mankind's best qualities?

He remembers this moment most vividly on his insomniac nights with Lluvia, when he is too haunted by questions to sleep. How many pivotal decision-making moments does one have in their life? Is this now one of them? He wonders what Merton would advise him to do. Should he regard his guilt in lovemaking as a sign that he should return to the monastery and make good on his vow to know God? Would they ever take him back?

14

Johnson's desk is as expansive as a Kansas plain. Everything about the man is massive. His abundant bright white hair. His muscular outstretched hand. His broad smile. The metrics are clearly different in Johnson's patrician world. They shake.

"Good to see you, Niall. How are you adjusting? I imagine teaching here must be a big change from monastic life."

"You might say." Niall chuckles. He's unsure how much to elaborate. He likes Johnson but is not naïve about the man's power. He's not going to confess to being overwhelmed by his students, especially when he doesn't know why Johnson has summoned him.

"I won't keep you guessing. A student of yours paid me a visit yesterday."

"Oh?" He doesn't have to ask who.

"Colton Chadwick."

"He doesn't think much of me."

"He says you asked the class to write songs."

"Yes."

"He thought it was busywork that had nothing to do with history. I want you to know I'm reporting what he said, not what I think."

"It was a way of getting them engaged. The Gettysburg Address was a jumping off point."

Johnson nods. "A creative approach. That's exactly what I hired you for." He continues nodding as if his head has been carried away by a restless sea. The silence isn't comforting. "It's what everyone should be doing, looking for unconventional ways to challenge the students . . . But Colton was, well, upset by the assignment."

"He didn't do it."

"I understand you told him he had to stay for detention."

"He didn't do that either."

"He reported to me that he felt you were picking on him. Because he's white. Again, his words, not mine."

"He hadn't done the work, so I did what I would do with any student."

"There isn't any possibility you might have singled him out because he's white? He thinks you're obsessed with race."

Niall sighs. "No—I . . ."

"It's a touchy issue, as you know. These damn lawmakers think they can decide what we can and can't teach. Terribly difficult. Even under the best of circumstances, and we're hardly in the best of circumstances."

"I can't teach American History without discussing race. Especially with a curriculum that begins with the Civil War."

"Of course you can't. I would never ask you to do that. But you also can't be seen as favoring any group of students over any other students."

"I wouldn't do that. I hope I don't."

"The situation is complicated because of who Colton's parents are."

"You mean wealthy?"

"Not just run-of-the-mill wealthy. They're extremely influential. The number of boards they sit on, not only in the Tri-State area but across the country, is staggering. They could send Colton to any school they wanted—a donation would guarantee that—but they've placed him here, they've told me, as a form of Tough Love. To see if he can survive in a public school with a diverse, working-class population."

"How can they—? Do they live in the district?"

"Oh, no, they live in a palatial house a little farther west. One of their many houses. But they bought a small home here that they use for Colton's official address."

"Does Colton actually live there?"

"I don't know the particulars." He pauses and frowns down at his desk, his hands interlaced as if he's praying. Something in his posture suggests guilt or remorse.

"I told him I'd talk to you. I don't want you to alter what you're doing. Don't let him intimidate you. But do be mindful of not letting this blow up into something larger than it needs to be. Throw him a bone now and then. We don't want the school to get a reputation for punishing white students. In this climate that would be, well—catastrophic. And we don't want his parents getting defensive. That, too, could get ugly."

"I'll do my best."

"Let the monk in you lead the way." Johnson comes around from behind his desk and he pats Niall on the back. Niall wonders if this is a sayonara pat, the prelude to his firing. If it's a choice between Colton's influential parents and a former monk, Niall will be the loser, no matter how much Johnson likes what he's doing.

Outside, rush hour traffic rules, and the sun has already begun to set, its pink leaking over the western sky. Only a few cars remain in the parking lot. Niall has parked on the far side, adjacent to the street, and is surprised to see Trinity perched on his hood, assuming her relaxed, after-hours persona.

"How did it go with Johnson?"

"You remembered."

"It's kind of memorable—a colleague getting reamed by the principal."

"I wasn't reamed exactly. Just put on notice. Colton reported me—he said I was picking on him because he's white."

"Yawa, knee deep."

"Apparently his parents are not only wealthy, but very influential. Johnson's worried about alienating them. The way he patted my back made me feel . . . well, I could be on the chopping block. Even though I think he likes me."

"I know those back pats. I've had way too many of those noblesse, obliged pats . . . So are you?"

"Am I what?"

"Picking on him because he's white?"

"I don't know. He's so darn smug. I just wish he'd drop my class."

"Tell him he's failing."

"He doesn't care."

Shouts distract them. Post-practice athletes pour from the gymnasium door, pumped with adrenaline, fanning across the parking lot, hopping into cars and gunning off. It surprises Niall how many of these not-wealthy male students drive cars to school. Powerful engines as powerful phalluses.

Niall and Trinity watch, both entranced. Niall likes observing the students when they have no idea he's there. They occupy a world he'll never be able to touch; he can't remember ever being like them—he has come to think he never was.

"Do you know Colton's parents bought a house in the district so he can go to school here? For the official address."

"That doesn't surprise me. Another house is probably nothing to them. Rich people do things like that. Princeton taught me about the *anything-goes* behavior of rich people. Probably the most important thing I learned there."

The cars race each other, gunning their motors, ignoring the parking lot's white lines. A free-for-all. A black BMW with blacked-out windows draws close, slows. The driver's window rolls down. Colton is at the wheel, another guy beside him. Niall and Colton's faces are within two feet of one another.

"Hey, Mr. O!" Colton brings the car to a full stop. "How're you doing? "

Niall nods. "This is Ms. White. She teaches math."

"I know Ms. White. Everyone knows Ms. White. I'm Colton. Or should I say, Mr. Chadwick," he laughs.

"Hey there, Colton," Trinity says.

"Are you two doing something cool for Halloween?"

Trinity guffaws.

"I don't think that's our thing," Niall says.

"Too bad. Best night of the year and you two would make a good pair. Anyway, see you in class."

Colton speeds off, Niall and Trinity watching in silence.

"There you go," Niall finally says. "That's him."

"Looks like he's fond of you," Trinity says.

Niall sighs. "My luck."

15

There were twenty-three brothers altogether: Brother Martin with the stutter, in his fifties, one of the younger ones; Brother Gregory in his eighties and slipping into dementia; Brother Joseph, not young himself, who shepherded Gregory here and there. There were Brothers Michael and Stephen and Simon. They were all elderly. There was Brother Basil who was in charge of the library, and Abbot Jerome, both in their mid-sixties perhaps, and Brother Francis, also in his sixties, and Thomas, in his early fifties, one of the two youngest along with Martin. And the others whose names it took Niall a while to learn. All of them were gentle, gracefully aging men who Niall both knew and did not know at all. He yearned to learn more about where they'd come from, what their lives had been like before they heard the call of God. He would have loved to know how that call had come to them, if it had been anything at all like his own gradual, then tumbling, experience. And what did they struggle with now? That he wanted to know more than anything else.

He studied their faces, the remarkably few lines inscribed by all their years of studying and working and praying. He had no idea how old most of them had been when they arrived here. Sometimes, when he was working side-by-side with a brother, he would try to initiate talk. But the conversations only went so far before work interrupted, or the other brother would hesitate, as if summoning the past was unseemly, perhaps disturbing. Maybe Niall was too new to be trusted yet, or too young, though Brother Francis didn't seem to think so. The brothers always closed the conversations subtly, with benign smiles that seemed to say, *No offense.*

Sometimes mysterious things happened. A community disruption. Niall would sense a break in the rhythm of things, a cleavage in the metronomic regularity of the hours. A hiccough. A pause. It was similar to the way he always knew when a sickness was coming over him, a not-rightness in his body, but in this case the general atmosphere was subtly altered. His premonition was always followed by one of the brothers vanishing for a while, a period of days, or sometimes weeks, or even months, and everyone noticed, but no one discussed it directly. The Abbot always asked them to pray. *Let us keep Brother Joseph—or Simon or Basil—in our prayers,* he would say obtusely. A health crisis or a death in the family, Niall usually assumed, but no one ever specified, and Niall wondered whether prayer of this nonspecific nature could ever be useful. Shouldn't prayer be specific and focused? He craved the personal. He missed it.

Six months of his postulancy had gone by, and he had affirmed to the Abbot that he was ready to move forward. "I believe you are," the Abbot agreed. "I believe you have calmed down and your commitment has grown." The brief ceremony, exclusively for him, took place in the chapel before the midday meal. There was some praying, some chanting, then the Abbot dressed him in his new robes, pristine white with a white scapular to distinguish him from the other brothers whose brown scapulars indicated they had taken permanent vows. Over the next two years, Niall would move closer to permanent vows, learning more about theology and delving more deeply into *The Rule of St. Benedict*. His new name was Brother Anselm, not either of the two saint names— Patrick and Andrew—which he had submitted to the Abbot, but a name the Abbot had selected for him. Anselm was an eleventh-century saint, a famed and still-respected scholar who was known for his writings on the nature and mysteries of faith.

Niall stood beside the Abbot at the dais looking out at the other brothers. He closed his eyes and repeated his new name to himself, *Anselm, Anselm, Anselm,* as the others raised their voices in song, anointing him with the gift of their music and claiming him as (almost) one of their own. God was wreathed around him, and Niall-Anselm knew he was at last in the right place, and he felt he could remain there at the dais forever, floating in the incandescence of divine love. When the music ended, he opened his eyes and smiled broadly, spontaneously, a bit foolishly he would later think, hoping the other brothers felt the full force of his love coming back at them.

As they filed out, several of the brothers touched his shoulder as if to bless him. Outside, in the middle of the gusty March wind, Brother Francis embraced him. Then Thomas gave him a stiff embrace. They all ate their lunch of potato soup in silence, and Niall was buoyed by the ritual and tranquility that accompanied his new membership; he would no longer have to worry about standing out in his puffy red jacket. Lunch concluded; they returned to their chambers for an hour of private prayer and study before the afternoon's work.

Back in his room, he laid on his bed, looking down at the white sea of his robes, feeling transformed. He was a monk now for real—he was Brother Anselm. He recalled how he had once felt donning his Boy Scout uniform for the first time. He'd loved the way it announced his identity to the world. He was in the Boy Scouts for only a year, was eager to quit after a few months because his pack leader, a former Marine, was mean and made them do pushups if they did the slightest thing wrong, but he had hated giving up that uniform. He wondered why the Abbot hadn't chosen one of the names he had suggested. Perhaps because the Abbot still thought of him as a scholar, although he wasn't a scholar anymore. Anselm was a more distinctive name than the ones he had suggested, and he felt privileged to follow Anselm's example by exploring the mysteries of faith.

He knew he should be praying, but his mind was too busy for prayer. He needed a poem to calm his overactive brain. Rumi maybe—Rumi's work always had a calming effect. So many lines of Rumi's had made an impression on him. *"Every holy person seems to have a different doctrine and practice, but there's really only one work."*

He reached for his mother's poetry book, *The Solace of Poetry,* but it wasn't there. It had been shelved between his Bible and *The Rule of St. Benedict.* He searched on the windowsill, on his bedside table, in his desk drawer, under the bed, under the covers. There were no other places to look. The book was gone. He lay back down, noting the smudges of dirt already on his new robes from kneeling on the floor.

Anselm. Brother Anselm. Saint Anselm. Saints and monks named after saints do not sweat the small stuff. They do not leap to possibly false conclusions. They do not get angry or hold grudges.

However. There was no doubt in his mind about the culprit. There were many hours where he had been absent from his chamber and Thomas could have snuck in. The thought burned him. It was only a book, and he might have been asked to relinquish the book anyway. Still, the anger festered.

"*Steal* is a strong word, Brother Anselm. How can you be sure of this?" The Abbot wore his usual benign look, but since Niall had learned about the familial relationship between the Abbot and Brother Thomas, Niall had come to understand the man was more complicated than he had thought, someone who honored family loyalties as well as loyalty to God. Was this a good thing? Did those loyalties ever conflict? He wasn't sure.

"Because I know he doesn't like me."

"Don't be silly. Of course he likes you. Why would you impute these bad feelings to him?"

"The way he looks at me, it's . . ."

"Brother Anselm, you're a man of God now. It's your duty to put such thoughts aside and be guided by love. It doesn't matter what Brother Thomas thinks of you. And obsessing in this way will hold you back."

"I know, but he came into my room . . . and he took my book, the book my mother gave me and . . ."

"*Your* book. *Your* room. You must move beyond this possessive way of thinking, this attachment to things. Haven't we discussed this before? I'll give you a text to contemplate during *Lectio Divina*. You will work on this, right? Promise me you'll work on this, Brother Anselm."

You approve of what has happened? Niall was tempted to say. *Is it perfectly fine for any brother to enter another brother's room and take what is there? Or do you only approve because it's been done by your own nephew?*

There was, of course, no way to say this, so instead he nodded, a mute promise to work against attachment. He left the Abbot's office quickly, knowing there was no support to be found there.

He had memorized some of the poems, and he tried to resurrect them, but his memory was blocked by the grudge he couldn't release.

A copy of the text he was supposed to study appeared on his desk: Matthew 6:19-21.

Do not lay up for yourselves treasure on earth, where moth and rust destroy and where thieves break in and steal, but lay up for yourselves treasure in heaven, where neither moth nor rust destroy and where thieves do not break in and steal. For where your treasure is, then your heart will be also.

A book, Niall kept telling himself. *It was only a book.* It was hard to regard a book as a ruinous earthly distraction when books were conduits of thought and God's word. It wasn't the same as hoarding money or jewels. As for heaven and its treasures, he had no opinion about that, no picture of heaven at all. He hadn't fully signed on to a belief in heaven—he was simply trying to negotiate this life on Earth.

Let it go, Niall—it's only a book.

16

They're walking from the car to the realtor's office on a brisk, blue-sky Saturday five days before Halloween. Lluvia slips her feathery hand into his. Dressed in fall colors—yellow skirt, orange top, red jacket—she's bouncing and humming, happy to be spending the day with him, happy to be thinking about sharing a house, content with the world and her place in it. Infected by her, he dips in and out of happiness himself—this must be what vacations are like, allowing anxious thoughts to dissipate.

Vacations have never figured prominently in his life—his parents never had the money or the interest in taking time off from work, and the idea of vacations was an anathema in the monastery—but hanging out with Lluvia has suggested to him what he's been missing. The rose-colored glasses feeling. The devil-may-care feeling. He could get used to this no-worry living.

Still, every once in a while, his mind wanders back to his workaday life. The meeting with Johnson has made him tiptoe around Colton, letting Colton get away with his sneering attitude and doing no work at all. That can't possibly be the right approach for making him feel okay about his whiteness. It bothers Niall to consider that maybe he *has* been treating Colton differently because he's white. But if he has, how can he change that? He needs to figure this out before he meets with Colton's mother, who has also requested a meeting.

Beverly, the realtor, sits at the helm of her lemon Cadillac like the buff debonair captain of a cruise ship. She gets out to shake hands, hyperventilating friendliness. "What cute lovebirds you two are! So good to meet you, Mr. Santos. Your wife has been telling me about you. You teach high school, I understand? You're one brave man!"

Your wife? Mr. Santos? Has Beverly jumped to conclusions or has Lluvia said they were married? Lluvia glances at him and shrugs in apology.

"I'm surviving so far."

Beverly hurries them into her car. "Lots to do today!"

Lluvia sits in the front, Niall in the back. The white leather seat he settles on would make a fine living room couch. A kewpie doll dangles from the rearview mirror, exuding the scent of vanilla.

"I have five places lined up, and we can see more if you've got the energy."

The Cadillac's superior suspension skims along the rutted streets like a posh baby carriage. They pass modest beach houses, interspersed with some older, bigger ones, Victorians that would be impressive had they not lapsed into shabbiness. He wonders what kind of house Colton's parents bought for him and whether he ever stays there. A high school boy with a house of his own—there's something deeply wrong with that.

Beverly, veteran saleswoman, is working on Lluvia.

"If you do the math, you'll find out that in the long run it's more economical to own than rent. For a young couple like you, if you buy now you'll be free and clear long before retirement, and then you'll have some discretionary funds for great vacations, remodeling, that kind of thing.

"So—with that in mind, I have one starter house to show you, after we see some of the rentals. I don't mean to be pushy, but it's perfect for your needs, with a remodeled garage apartment that would be perfect for your mother, Lluvia."

Lluvia glances at the back seat. "What do you think, Niall? Shall we have a look?"

He shrugs. "Why not?" This is Lluvia's arrangement, and he already resolved to be agreeable. He wishes he were back on the sidewalk holding her warm feather of a hand, feeling that vacation feeling again.

He glances out, and there on the sidewalk is his student Rania, walking hand-in-hand with another girl he doesn't recognize. He waves madly, but Rania doesn't see him and they pass her quickly. His students, he suddenly realizes, are always on his mind now, parked there like feisty squatters who periodically demand his attention. The ones he likes exist alongside the ones doesn't like, taking up equal amounts of real estate.

The rentals blur together, similar as they are: meek exteriors, square rooms with recent paint jobs filled with the vaguely fungal scent of desperation and the fraught silence of quick departures. The odd hanger has been left behind, a "Life is Good" refrigerator magnet, nothing egregious, and everything is Comet-clean, but nevertheless he finds these houses inexplicably sad. He parades behind Lluvia dutifully, marveling at her ability to find details to rave about. The closets! A laundry room! A garage with built-in shelves! He always lived in apartments and has never evaluated houses before. He tries to think of questions so he doesn't appear to be such a dullard but, unlike his father, he knows nothing about the infrastructure of buildings, wiring and plumbing and roofs, the very things his father excelled in. His deficits, he sees, are far greater than the cultural trends he has failed to notice— there are numerous important details of the physical world he knows nothing about too.

The starter house, a few blocks from the beach, is on a lot of scrappy grass and sand. Wind and salt have shorn the façade. It appears not only empty but abandoned, as if it was on its way to collapse before some dubiously-effective intervention: a slapdash paint job inside and out, executed without proper scraping and sanding and priming, and the installation of second-hand appliances, plywood cabinets, a plastic shower stall. Niall may not know much about houses, but he knows this would be a foolhardy investment. The remodeled garage apartment is the only asset, but he doubts it has been properly insulated; Rocio would surely be cold there in the winter months.

"We should have brought a tape measure," Lluvia says.

She measures the perimeter of the master bedroom, placing one foot in front of the other, then flattening her back against one wall. "We could put a bed here, and we'd wake up to the sun rising over that little sliver of water!" she says.

Right, he thinks, *a sliver, not a full view.* When did he become a glass-half-empty person? He nods, incapable of expressing himself with Beverly's watchful eye on them; he can see how eager she is to capitalize on Lluvia's enthusiasm and urge them toward an offer.

It is dusk by the time Beverly returns them to Lluvia's car. The best part of the day is gone, along with every shred of vacation feeling. Lluvia doesn't start the car, but swivels to him, sensing his mood. "I know it's just a shell of a house now, but we could do so much with it."

"Maybe." But with what? He has no savings, and she doesn't have much either. They would have to borrow, at high interest rates, and borrowing scares him, making them beholden to institutions for who knows how long.

He would love to be as excited as Lluvia is, but all he feels is eviscerated. What bothers him about physical objects is how immutable they are; once he's taken a disliking to an object, including a house, he has a hard time seeing it in a better light. He didn't like that house at all, though he couldn't bring himself to say so, knowing how it would dampen Lluvia's enthusiasm. He can't imagine they could do much to improve it. It had bad juju, or bad karma, or bad—whatever. It seemed like a house with an impure soul. He pictures being there, blocks from the shore, battered by wind and salt air, seeing the elements as vicious attackers, confined inside with Lluvia and Flora and Rocio and being stricken by claustrophobia, which no one would understand, and which would seem mean-spirited.

"I just don't think it's a good investment," he says. He fixates on the nobs of the radio which Lluvia says haven't been working for years. Both of their cars, his Volvo and her Ford, are almost twenty years old and close to giving up. They need functioning cars more than they need a house.

"It's okay. We can keep looking. Beverly has made up a long list for us."

"I don't know."

"What don't you know?"

"I don't think I'm ready."

"You're not ready to buy, or you don't want to live with me? With us? You don't want to marry me? Let's be clear about this. Tell me what you're thinking."

"It's not that. I love you—you know I love you. But living together? And marriage? They're such big steps."

"You think I come with too much baggage, don't you?" She lays her hand on his thigh, presses lightly on the denim, a request to explain himself. "You can tell me—I won't fall apart."

But I might, he thinks.

17

Trinity knows how to act around rich people—Princeton taught her that—and she has offered to give Niall some tips for his upcoming meeting with Colton's mother. They're in the parking lot at the end of the school day, as has become their frequent habit, leaning against her car. Hers, along with his, are the last to vacate the parking lot.

"Start off by saying something flattering about her son—you know, butter her up."

"It might be hard to find something honest to say."

"Anything will do—it doesn't have to be honest. But don't be the least bit obsequious. Let her know you know what you're doing—you don't want her treating you like you're her servant."

"Even though I am."

"Bullshit. Watch your body language—you know, don't slouch—and don't let your sentences trail off. When she arrives, shake her hand firmly, and tell her where to sit. Make it clear from the start who's piloting the ship."

"Hah! You know what we were told in the monastery—part of *The Rules of St. Benedict*: 'Express humility in your bodily posture.'"

"God, no. Don't do that! In a conversation like this, that's suicide."

"How did you learn all this? When I was your age, I didn't know anything. I still don't." "I've learned what I've had to learn . . . Hey, what if I pop in after a while and ask to talk to you for a minute, pretending it's urgent. You get up and confer with me, and I'll have a chance to eyeball her and give you some on-the-spot pointers. My presence, being the imposing black girl I am, might give you some extra clout. She might even be scared of me."

At 3:30 p.m., Niall positions himself at his desk, reminding himself that he is commander of this room, his home for the last two months. Looking at it through Mrs. Chadwick's eyes, it appears cheerless, despite all he has done to fix it up. Nial wonders if she knows about the cash-strapped state of the school that has lent a wearied look to everything: the map of the world Scotch-taped to the wall, its edges curling; the tables with their chipped laminate veneers covered so regularly with graffiti that the Clorox used to clean them has left ghostly palimpsests; the crack in the corner of one of the large windows. He has no doubt she will spot these things immediately. They don't reflect on him directly, though she'll probably think they do. But this is the school she chose for her son.

The authoritative clip-clop of heels precedes her standing in the open doorway, swashbuckling, taller than he. Saffron suede jodhpurs; salmon silk shirt; brown knee-high, high-heeled boots; chunks of rough gold in her ears, displayed as if she panned it herself. Slung over one arm are a matching handbag and beige leather car coat. Her skin is bronzed, her auburn hair shoulder-length and highlighted with streaks of gold. At first glance, she could be a billionaire Wyoming cowgirl.

After a brief pause in which she scans the classroom, she sweeps through the doorway. He rises, extends the firm handshake Trinity advised. They exchange names. Niall O'Malley. Suzanne Chadwick. Her voice is melodic, shaded by an accent that veers toward British. He gestures to the table where he has readied his gradebook and some teaching materials, and they sit. She glances around the room again.

"Ah, school. Schools always smell the same everywhere, don't they? The same as when I was coming up."

He nods. She sounds neutral, even friendly. He needs to back off from stereotyping. "Did you go to school around here?"

"I grew up in the Boston area."

"So did I. Where did you go to school?"

"The Windsor School."

He knows of the place, a private school with a reputation for educating the elite.

"And you?" she says.

"A small parochial school in Charlestown."

Ah, he sees her thinking, *Catholic.*

"I didn't expect you to be so young."

He shrugs. He doesn't feel young, not as young as Trinity, not as young as he felt in the monastery, but Mrs. Chadwick must be in her late forties, possibly fifties, so yes, to her he is young.

"Do you have kids?"

"No."

"I understand you were once in the monastery."

He wonders if Colton told her this, or if she learned from other sources. "Yes."

"Do you mind my asking why you left?"

He should be asking *her* questions, taking command. "It's a long story, but basically it wasn't the life for me."

"And this life is? Cooped up all day with adolescents?" She laughs. "I wouldn't be able to take it. I raised three sons and a daughter—Colton is the youngest—and it was pure joy with them until they reached adolescence and then, more days than not, I wanted to strangle them."

I often think of strangling your son too. "It's different, I think, when they don't belong to you," he says. "So, what are your concerns about Colton?"

She smiles with closed lips, the first sign she isn't entirely well-disposed to him. "I don't know that it's Colton I'm concerned about. Frankly, I'm wondering why your class is the only one he's having trouble with. He's doing fine in his other classes. He'll never be a stellar student—his dyslexia, you know—but at least he's passing and learning a few things. And he's not as angry as he was. It was a good choice to move him here. But in your class, there seems to be—an impasse, shall we say."

"He hasn't done any of the work, if that's what you mean."

"But why hasn't he? I think there's a reason, and I think you know what it is."

"I don't. Please tell me."

"I think you're letting your political views—which seem to be prominently on display here"—she gestures to his wall of photographs largely focused on civil rights, John Lewis, Martin Luther King Jr.—"get in the way of your teaching."

"How do you mean?"

"Look, how many weeks have you spent on Frederick Douglass?"

"His speeches and writings are a very important—and often ignored—part of our history."

"I never learned about Frederick Douglass when I was in school, and I don't think I've suffered for it. In certain places in this country, it's becoming illegal to teach these things."

"Not here in New Jersey. I never learned about Frederick Douglass in high school either, and I think that's a problem."

"The problem, if you'll excuse me for saying so, is that you're making the students feel bad about themselves. Colton and the other white students in your class feel undervalued and threatened."

"Why do you say that, Mrs. Chadwick?"

"They feel guilty about being white. They've told me. Not just Colton, but some of his friends too. But Colton especially. You probably think I'm echoing the news media, but Colton really feels this way."

"Colton feels guilty? He hasn't said so."

"He's too shy to tell you. He thinks you *want* him to feel guilty."

"That couldn't be further from the truth."

"Colton says your girlfriend is black. He thinks that's why you're teaching all this race stuff. That you have an agenda."

A chill comes over him. He looks to the door—where is Trinity? "I don't believe Colton has met my girlfriend."

"He's seen you two together . . . Look, Niall—may I call you Niall? Niall, my son is more sensitive than he may appear. He has very low self-esteem in part because his older siblings are such high achievers. I know he exhibits a lot of attitude sometimes, but beneath his attitude is a delicate ego. He's very easily bruised. That's why he became a wrestler, so he could defend himself against the nastiness in the world. A little protection, you know?"

Protection? Colton needs protection? What a laughable thought. Niall's logical mind is sluggish, what are his priorities? Should he try to quash the rumor about him and Trinity? *Could* he? He feels feverish, frigid. Bile burns his alimentary canal. He mustn't explode at her.

"My husband is hard on Colton. They go head-to-head a lot. You know, male egos. So, I try to compensate by being kind and helping Colton out however I can. I'm sure I coddle him too much, but that's what mothers do. Good mothers, that is. So, the long and the short of it is, I'm asking that you join me in being a little kinder to Colton. Help me nurture him and feed his ego a little to help him find a place for himself. The world isn't easy these days for a guy like Colton." She spears Niall with a direct gaze. "Are you willing to help me out?"

Feed his ego? Niall hesitates. He wishes Trinity would show up so he could rise and put his arm around her, saying, *Meet my girlfriend.* But Trinity is not here. He curls his fingers into fists. If he were a parent, would he be advocating for his kid in this way, doing everything he could, even if his kid was an arrogant lazy bum like Colton? Would he want to feed such a child's overblown ego if that child were his own? Mrs. Chadwick, Suzanne, is watching him like a poker player, a soupçon of desperation undermining her resolute expression.

"Do you mind if I ask you something, Mrs. Chadwick?"

"Go ahead."

"Why exactly did you choose to send Colton here—to a public school that isn't exactly known for being the best around? Don't you worry it will hold him back?"

She recrosses her legs, takes a roll of mints from her purse, offers him one, which he refuses, pops one into her mouth, and snaps her purse closed. She stares over his shoulder, then looks back at him, sucking her mint audibly, drilling him with her gaze.

"This is extremely confidential. I don't want it getting out. No one knows but Dr. Johnson. Colton went through some trouble in his last school. He always likes to push boundaries, be a bit of a provocateur, you know? And like most adolescents, he especially wants to push his parents.

"Niall, you must know we are good people, Hugh and I. You might have gotten the wrong impression about us. What I said about Colton feeling like he's supposed to feel bad because he's white—I know that isn't politically correct. I'm not stupid. But we have the right values, my husband and I. We like and support black people. We really do. We have given more money to black organizations and schools and job training and what-not than almost anyone in the country. And we have always been this way."

She pauses.

"So, Colton . . ." She pauses again, looking over Niall's shoulder again. "Colton got mixed up with the wrong people at his last school. He was clearly trying to provoke Hugh and me. He was doing what kids do. But he pushed it too far. So we thought a school like this would be a wakeup call. So many races and religions. And I think it has been." She pauses. "So . . ." She chews the remainder of her mint loudly and takes out a monogrammed handkerchief to dab her lips.

He watches without saying a word. Her nerves have given him the upper hand.

"I'm not following you, Mrs. Chadwick. What happened exactly?"

"I don't think the details matter. Colton made some bad choices and he's paid for it. He's ready to move on and take charge of his life. Become an upstanding citizen with good values."

Niall nods, hoping for more, but she has folded herself back up, done being candid.

She reaches for her car coat. "Have you read his letter?'

"What letter?"

"He wrote you a letter, expressing some of his feelings and saying how he doesn't want to fail and would like to do better. I guess he forgot to give it to you. I'll remind him to bring it tomorrow." She gathers her handbag and rises. "Thank you for hearing me out. I'm glad we see eye-to-eye about this, Niall. Let's stay in touch. And let me reiterate: All of this is confidential. I hope I can trust you."

Trust me with what? Niall wants to say, but she's already moving to the door.

Trinity is waiting for him at his car. They watch Mrs. Chadwick zipping away in her black BMW, the same car they've seen Colton driving. He stands beside Trinity, knowing and not caring that he's adding fodder to the rumor they are boyfriend and girlfriend.

"I came by your room, but I couldn't get myself to go in. It looked like you were too heavily into it. And women like that— for all my supposed strategies, they still intimidate me. I hope you didn't need rescuing."

"She told me something supposedly confidential, but I have no idea what it is."

"She looks like a piece of work."

"She said she loves black people and gives them a lot of money."
They both laugh.

The next day Colton enters the classroom and slides an envelope onto Niall's desk. He nods then heads to his usual table.

Today's topic: Douglass's speech, "What to the Slave is the Fourth of July?"

"I've never been able to relate to the Fourth of July," Rania says. "It's clearly not intended for anyone with brown skin."

"Okay—so this essay makes a good point, yeah," Dominic says. "But it's so repetitive. Slavery sucks—end of story."

"Do you think what he says has any bearing on today?"

Of course, some of them say, but they can't elaborate.

The discussion limps along. Niall feels himself holding back, checking everything he says for how Colton—and all the other white students—might be hearing it. Colton's envelope flashes in and out of his peripheral vision. Finally, the class is over, the room empty. He picks up the envelope. *Mr. Niall O'Malley* is written in neat block letters. It occurs to him this is the first time he has seen anything Colton has written.

The letter inside is on lined three-hole paper that has been ripped from a notebook, still ragged with hanging chads. The handwriting is a nearly illegible scrawl and doesn't match the writing on the front of the envelope, which suggests his mother's participation.

Dear Mr. O'mally,

I know you hate me and it herts my feelings. I didn't do anything wrong. this class is crushing my sole. You say I dont do the work but I wuld do it if it wasnt all about how im sposed to feel gilty. I cant help the color I was born and I have nothing against black people.

You migt not know but the way you teech this class isnt good. it is the only class that makes me feel bad . Im teling you now so maybe you can change. Just because your girlfriend is black doesen't mean you should teach us only about black people. I wunder if yur meenness comes from you being irish. The Irish people killed eachother for meny years. You shudnt crush a yung person, everyone says that. I have big potenshul let me tell you. its yur job to bring that out. Ive never felt so bad in a class before.

Colton
Ps pleez email my mother so she knows you got this

Niall reads the letter several times, taking note of its odd mix of vulnerability and bravado. It's hard to gauge the letter's authenticity. Clearly, it was penned by Colton—whose literacy is shockingly subpar—but could his mother possibly have dictated what he should write? Niall is stuck on the first line—*I know you hate me*—because, though hate may be too strong a word, Niall does dislike Colton. And the suggestion that Niall is mean because he's Irish?! Is that his mother talking? Niall is not Irish—he is one hundred percent American. And the idea that he is foisting his love of black people on the class because he has a black girlfriend—how can Niall possibly address that? He hopes Johnson will tell him more particularly what Colton did to get kicked out of his last school.

He pictures Colton sprawled on the bed of his spacious room in his parents' mansion-house, a room with all the newest high-tech devices of a rich boy. Gaming computer, tablet, phone, TV, speakers, ear buds, athletic gear, weights, and punching bag. His bed would be a queen or a king, covered with a quilt in a masculine navy blue or brown, sham covers to match. He sees Colton contemplating the letter his mother wants him to write to his history teacher. He does not want to write the letter but, unable to wiggle out of it, he has finally given in. He can't procrastinate any longer and hurls himself to standing, rummages in his backpack for notebook paper, yanks off a piece, not caring that he's ripped it messily. He grabs a pen and a book and lies back down on the bed on his belly, propped on his elbows, paper on book. He writes whatever comes to his mind, trying to remember the points his mother said he should cover. He loves his mom, but she has gone overboard here; it pains him to write this shit to his history teacher, a loser of a guy, a pipsqueak and weakling, a former monk, for god's sake, a man Colton could pin in a nanosecond.

18

It was almost a year into his Novitiate. After lunch he prayed at his desk. His concentration was improving, but his understanding of prayer was still sketchy. He prayed for his mother, hoping she was not too lonely. He prayed for Liam who moved through life grabbing things quickly. Too quickly, it seemed to Niall, though that was for God to judge. He prayed for himself, that the ill will he knew still resided in his soul would not prevail. He prayed for Francis whose health he worried about. He tried to pray for Thomas, as he knew he should, but when he did, his concentration evaporated.

Thankfully, Thomas had been less of a problem for the previous few months. He didn't try to start conversations, and nothing more had disappeared from Niall's chamber. Maybe the Abbot had admonished him? Thomas still kept his eye on Niall, but Niall had learned to blur his gaze and pretend he didn't notice.

The light in the west-facing window of his chamber mesmerized him as it transfigured the landscape. Pink. Orange. Violet. Silver. Gold. God resided in that light. He *was* that light. Because of that, Niall often prayed with his eyes open, receiving the warmth of God through his retina, hoping it would increase his understanding.

That day the snowy landscape was a silvery blue. Perfectly tranquil. He had always loved winter, the cleansing clamor of the cold air, the warmth of a fire, the invitation to hibernate. He closed his eyes, bowed his head, and prayed for his mother.

The floorboards creaked. He turned. Thomas stood in the doorway. His black beard. His bulbous lips. His unblinking blue eyes. His presence plundered the room. Niall turned away, tamping his annoyance. This couldn't be proper, entering without even knocking. Wasn't it against the rules? Though he couldn't remember reading such a rule.

He corralled his breath, turned to the doorway again. Thomas acknowledged Niall with a nod, but still didn't leave. His gaze raked the corners of the room, commanding the space as if it were his own.

"Please," Niall begged, turning away again and lowering the crown of his head to his desk. *Breath in. Breathe out. Find the quiet of a cave.* Moments later a breeze swiped his cheek as the door clicked shut. Thomas was gone.

The Abbot made light of it. "Keep counsel with yourself, Brother Anselm. Leave the other brothers to themselves."

"But they don't keep to themselves. He entered without knocking."

"Did that harm you?"

"He interrupted my prayer."

"Many things interrupt prayer, Brother Anselm. That is the nature of human life. You must master these interruptions. And speak to him if it bothers you. It will be fine, I assure you. I think you worry too much."

"But why? Why does he do this?"

"Try to let it go and follow God. He will tell you that some things are not to be understood."

Niall cornered Thomas outside the library. "Why do you watch me?" he asked. He tried not to sound pleading or excessively annoyed. But he was, of course, annoyed.

"I watch you?"

"You came into my room without knocking. Everywhere I go, you're watching me. What do you want from me?"

Thomas turned his gaze skyward and tugged on his full upper lip. Niall wished he hadn't posed such a direct question, worried about an honest answer. Sex with Thomas was the last thing Niall wanted. The thought was abhorrent.

"You're new and vulnerable, Brother Anselm. What I see in you is my young self."

Like Thomas? *Hogwash.* He wasn't at all like Thomas, had never been, and never would be. Without excusing himself, he walked away.

19

The fifth period students are moaning and groaning about having to do ten-page research papers, due before the holiday break. Most of them have never written papers of more than five pages, and he knows he will have to hold their hands through the process. He has divided them into small groups to brainstorm topics. They are super chatty today. Some of them wear parts of Halloween costumes—fairy wings, tutus, donkey ears, glitzy caps.

There's a tapping on the peekaboo window of his classroom door. Trinity. He opens the door and beckons her inside, but she resists, gesturing, urgent. "No," she whispers, reaching for his forearm to drag him into the hallway.

He steps out, "I'll be back," he says over his shoulder, and he shuts the door behind him.

"Follow me." Trinity is already flying down the hallway, her stride so long and quick he can barely keep up. He should go back and say something more to his students about what to do in his absence, but Trinity's urgency has his head scrambled. They travel the length of his corridor, turn left at the lobby, and traverse the length of her corridor. "What?" he keeps saying. "What?" They enter her empty classroom. She closes the door, locks it. "Stay there."

She approaches her desk slowly as if something dangerous resides there. Three feet from her desk she crouches and runs her forefinger across the floor. She returns to him, extending her finger.

"Look." She waggles her finger.

"What?"

"Feel it."

Timidly he touches her finger. "Grease?"

"Vaseline. It doesn't smell like anything. Fucking *petroleum jelly.* It goes all around my desk. Look. Follow me."

She circles her desk, crouching here and there to slide her finger along the floor again, encouraging him to do the same, occasionally tiptoeing over the slick surface.

"I came in here after lunch and I went flying. See. I could have broken something." She turns to show him the grease spot on the back of her skirt, and rolls back her blouse sleeve to show him an elbow bruise. "Assholes."

His attention is hash. "You think someone spread this intentionally?"

"No, it just magically appeared. *Of course* someone put it here."

"But who? Do you have enemies?"

She rolls her eyes. "When were you born? Everyone's my enemy until they've proven they're not."

"What will you do?"

"Clean it up and get on with things."

"Pete will do it for you. Don't do it yourself—call him."

"No way. This is between you and me, okay? No one else. Now go, get out. Go back to your classroom."

"You're going to tell Johnson, aren't you?"

"Fuck no."

"You have to tell him."

"I don't need that drama. If they see I'm upset it only gratifies whoever did it."

"Why did you tell me?"

"You're my witness if I ever need one. If anyone suggests I'm being paranoid."

"What if *I* tell Johnson?"

"Don't you dare. I should never have told you. Now get out of here."

"Take a picture at least."

"What's to see?"

"Yeah, I guess." Still, he snaps a photo with a bit of gleam on the floor.

"Get back to your class. And if you tell Johnson . . ."

"We'll talk about this later, right?"

She waves him off, clearly annoyed. The soles of his running shoes bleat on the polished floors as he heads back to his room. His gut is roiling; he's short of breath. He tries to connect the dots and find a target for his anger, but it eludes him. His students must be going berserk.

Twenty feet from his classroom door he slows, tries to collect himself. He's lost his train of thought, can't remember what he hoped to accomplish today. *Ah yes*—the small groups, their research papers. If he's lucky Rania will have kept them under control. He's only been gone a matter of minutes.

He peers through the peekaboo window. No one. He opens the door. The classroom is empty. Not a single student. Not Rania, not Camilla, not Mateo. They've all bailed.

20

The color and heat remain imprinted. He was only a small boy of five—how could such a tiny boy contain so much heat? But each time he thinks back he recalls that heat keenly, the way it originated in his chest and spread to his belly and limbs and scalp as he stood at his bedroom window and watched Liam and his mother walk down the sidewalk to the car, chatting happily without him. They were going to the ice cream parlor as a special treat because Liam had gotten perfect marks on his year-end report card. A special certificate had come home with a gold star on it saying what an excellent student Liam was.

Why was the world so unfair? Niall had done well in his kindergarten class too. He didn't have the same kind of marks to show for it because they didn't have those marks in kindergarten, but the teacher had said complimentary things. So why couldn't he have ice cream too? It didn't make sense, and Niall was mad. It wasn't the ice cream itself that made him so mad, it was the way Liam had stolen his mother, and they were walking hand-in-hand as if they, exclusively, belonged to each other, as if no other son existed, when Niall had always been sure that his mother belonged mostly to him.

He watched until they turned the corner and disappeared from sight, and still he stood there, heat spilling everywhere in his body, a combination of water and fire, singeing his limbs, bearing a yellow-orange color like the sun, but not gentle like the sun—mean, very mean.

It was a Saturday, and his father was downstairs doing the dishes from lunch. Usually his father worked on Saturdays, but not that day. It didn't occur to Niall to ask why. He didn't like being left alone with his father. His father wasn't unkind, but he didn't talk much, and Niall was awkward around him, having no idea what to say. Alone in the house, just the two of them, they both kept their distance.

Full of the heat, Niall left his post at the window and went to Liam's room. He hated everything about this neat room which proved that Liam was a better person than he was. He hated the perfectly made bed. He hated the right angles of the books in the shelves and the papers on the desk. He hated that all of Liam's clothes were put away, none of them clumped on the floor as Niall's clothes were. Displayed prominently on one side of the desk was the medieval LEGO castle Liam had received for his ninth birthday in May—hundreds of pieces he'd put together without help. The little helmeted soldiers kept watch over the lands below with their bayonets ready.

Niall seized one of the soldiers and rolled it between both hands. He snapped the soldier's tiny bayonet in two. He snapped the helmet off the soldier's head. He snapped the head off the body. He snapped the body in two and tossed the pieces to the floor. The yellow-orange serum inside him was boiling now as he ripped off the turrets, the tower, the drawbridge, the gate house. Snap. Snap. Snap. They came off so easily and the plastic broke easily too, especially when he stamped on it.

The castle lay in pieces on the floor. He had destroyed everything, crushing the soldiers and their ruined castle into sharp shards like shells whose edges dug into his bare feet. He skulked back to his room and hid under his covers and waited for the boiling feeling to subside. If he was lucky they wouldn't know it was him.

For months after that, he did anything Liam told him to do. *I'm sorry,* he said several times a day, until Liam told him to knock it off.

His mother bought him an inflatable punching bag in the shape of a waving clown. Bobo. She told him to punch Bobo when he was mad. The arrogant, self-satisfied thing popped back up at him with each punch, infuriating him all the more. He'd never liked clowns, and this clown was especially obnoxious with his jovial waving hand and electrified red hair. He kicked the stupid thing to a corner of his room where it leered at him in the night, so he shoved it into his closet, out of sight.

He didn't get mad all that often. Not really. When he did get mad most people didn't notice. It was an inside feeling, something he kept to himself. Like holding your breath or your pee—you did it with your muscles.

In third grade Mrs. Sargent punished him for whispering during a math test. She thought he might be cheating. He wasn't cheating, only whispering—why would he cheat when he was so good at math?—but she made him stay inside for recess and write: *It is wrong to whisper during tests.*

She ate her lunch while he wrote, powering through her sandwich with sucking sounds and keeping her mouth open in a way that would have irritated his father and now irritated him. *Keep your damned mouth closed,* his father would have said. Listening to those rude sounds made the injustice of the situation worse, and the heat came to him, settling into his body in the usual places. She excused herself to the ladies' room. "Stay right where you are. I know you're a good boy, Niall. I know this won't happen again."

As soon as she was out of the room the heat made him rise. He went to her desk and grabbed her yellow #2 pencil. He bit down on it hard, his tooth marks going deep, deeper, deeper, until he heard her snippety-snip, clippety-clop, high-heeled footsteps coming back down the hall, and he dropped the pencil and scurried back to his desk. Resuming her seat, she did not appear to notice the bitten pencil which lay exposed before her. If she saw it later, he never knew.

It was then, under Mrs. Sargent's watch, that he learned to direct his rage into invisible revenge.

21

After the final period of the day Niall joins the crush of exiting students and makes his way to Trinity's classroom. Peering through the door's small window he doesn't see her, but he enters anyway. She's not there; her coat isn't on its usual hook; she must be gone for the day. The air still carries the slightest perfumed scent of her—"Egyptian Goddess," she said the scent was called.

It's rare for her to leave so early. He approaches her desk, checks the floor and finds a thin layer of Vaseline still remaining. The wastebasket is overflowing with paper towels covered with gobs of the stuff. He thinks of calling Pete then realizes Pete will discover it anyway on his usual rounds.

Battling the outgoing tide of students again, he returns to his own classroom, ruing the state of the world. What is wrong with people? Even young people should know better. Was the Vaseline supposed to get a laugh, or was it malevolent? He hopes it was to get a laugh though he knows Trinity would say otherwise, and he suspects she's right.

He sits at his desk, wondering what kind of mood Trinity is in. He knows he would be furious if someone did something like that to him. It wouldn't be something he would remain quiet about. He packs up the stacks of papers he has to grade. He has fallen woefully behind—maybe tonight he can begin to catch up. He's having conferences soon about research papers with the students in three of his five classes. He already knows he's expecting a lot from them, maybe too much, but they need someone to hold a high bar for them. He looks forward to talking to them individually, getting to know them a little better. He texts Trinity: *You okay?* No answer.

When all traces of sunlight have disappeared from his window, he rises to go, dreading the long lonely night of grading ahead. The hallway lights have been turned off, the only illumination coming from the lobby. His footsteps sound menacing, even to him.

Someone else's footsteps are approaching from the south corridor. Just his luck that it's Colton, coming from wrestling practice, still dressed in his sleeveless red-and-yellow team jersey, his face and exposed arms slick with sweat.

"Well, well," Colton says sounding like some middle-aged pedant about to make a pronouncement, "imagine seeing you here."

Niall laughs. "Well, I do work here." He laughs again. "Maybe you can tell me why you and the rest of the class bailed on me today."

"You bailed first, I believe."

Colton is right, and Niall's infraction, as a teacher, is worse than the class's infraction. He wishes Colton's comebacks weren't always seeded with a touch of unwelcome truth, not to mention moral superiority.

"My brothers say that at college you're allowed to leave if the professor is ten minutes late. So we gave it eleven minutes." As Colton speaks his biceps pulse as if to say, *Don't mess with me.* A towel hangs from his backpack, and he uses it to wipe his face. "Well, I gotta go and get ready for tonight. Oh, wait, I've been meaning to show you something."

He swipes his phone and holds out a picture for Niall to examine: he and Trinity sitting on the hood of her car, their bottoms inches from one another, both of them laughing, her head thrown back, mouth open.

"Oh god, no." There is nothing overtly incriminating in the photo, except for the intimacy of shared laughter, and something embarrassing about the way he leans toward her, as if he's her acolyte.

"What? It's cute," says Colton.

"When did you take that?"

"Oh, I don't know. You two are always out there when I'm leaving practice, yucking it up."

"Would you mind deleting it?"

"Why? You're ashamed?"

"I'm not ashamed."

"Then what?"

"What are you going to do with it? I don't want you posting it. I have a girlfriend, you know, not Ms. White, and people might think . . ."

"Ah—you're two-timing? Don't worry. I won't do anything." Colton laughs and winks at Niall like some backroom power broker.

"Ms. White and I are just friends."

"Okay, if you say so." Another wink.

"Please don't spread any false rumors."

"Whatever. Anyway, I gotta go. I left my costume in my locker. Happy Halloween, Mr. O."

It's Halloween, of course. How can he have forgotten? His plan to use the evening for grading is foiled, as he has promised to go trick-or-treating with Flora and Lluvia. He watches Colton swagger off down the dim north corridor, lifting his tail of hair to wipe sweat from his tattooed shoulder. Pete is pushing his cleaning cart in the other direction, toward the lobby, and the two cross paths.

"Hey, Mr. Lopez, Happy Halloween," Colton says loudly, his voice carrying down the hallway as if he's speaking to Niall, not Pete.

"Happy Halloween to you too."

"Where's your costume? You should have a costume."

"I'm too old for that stuff. But you go have fun."

"Okay, I'll bring you some candy."

"Oh no, it's bad for me."

"Oh, Pete, once a year won't hurt. Everyone likes candy."

Pete laughs. He appears to know and like Colton, which makes Niall feel like a curmudgeon. Maybe Colton isn't really as bad as Niall has made him out to be. Just lazy. But Pete doesn't have to teach Colton.

Niall waves to Pete and hurries out the front door. He should have left earlier; he's due at Lluvia's in fifteen minutes for a quick bowl of soup before trick-or-treating.

22

When Niall was growing up, his Charlestown neighborhood went berserk on Halloween. Fires erupted in alleyways; Roman candles and bottle rockets exploded in the middle of the streets; big boys hurled eggs, smoke bombs, spinners, poppers. The cops would descend unexpectedly on motorcycles, sending the boys scuttling into houses and alleyways like so many cockroaches. Niall and Liam watched the commotion from their apartment windows. Their mother always took them trick-or-treating before dark at the homes of people they knew, where they were given plastic bags containing a few pieces of wrapped candy (one colleague of his mother's gave out apples and toothbrushes, which were quickly trashed), and they were always back home early before the older kids cut loose. Niall knew some kids his age who were allowed out after dark to join the mayhem, and Liam always begged to join too, but Niall was happy not to be part of the chaos. After observing the hijinks from his bedroom window for a while, he would cocoon himself under the covers, sucking his peanut M&M's one by one to make them last, awakening the next morning with chocolate-smeared teeth and bad breath, happy to be done with Halloween.

Niall trips along the slick street in a too-long brown monk's robe, rented on Flora's insistence from a costume shop. He left his white robes at the monastery, knowing he would have no use for them in secular life. An earlier rain has left puddles everywhere so his shoes and socks are soaked, his feet cold.

Flora is dressed as Charles Manson, with a strap-on dense brown beard and brown wig that makes for a somewhat credible facsimile of the man himself. She borrowed a shirt from Niall that covers most of her thighs, and she splattered it with red paint that is supposed to look like blood. She has been practicing her "wicked gaze" by widening her eyes and staring hard at people until they squirm in discomfort. Niall doesn't approve of this costume and all the attendant research Flora has done into Charles Manson and his nefarious deeds. Why learn prematurely about the most heinous behavior of human beings? But Lluvia has registered no objection, so Niall has kept his reservations to himself. Lluvia is dressed as a mermaid with a stuffed cotton fish tail made by Rocio, covered with blue-and-green-sequins. *Manson, Mermaid, Monk, the three Ms,* Flora has been saying to justify her insistence that he dress as a monk.

The proximity of the houses makes this a busy neighborhood for trick-or-treating. Posses of kids of all ages move in and out of the streetlights, like actors taking their spotlight then retreating. Lluvia speaks to many of them, stopping them to admire their costumes. "How clever," she tells someone dressed as a cell phone. "Beautiful," she says to a blonde-wigged goddess. "Terrifying," she says to a well-wrought witch with a gnarled nose made of putty.

Niall has not said more than a few words all evening. He can't shake his gloom, his worry about the rumor abroad that he and Trinity are an item, the multiple kinds of trouble this might cause. And how is he supposed to handle Colton and Colton's mother? The pussyfooting he's been doing around Colton feels wrong. The simmering has begun, the rising heat. He should quarantine himself before he does anyone harm.

Flora has announced her plan: They will travel five blocks on one side of the street, five blocks back on the other, hitting all the houses. So far she has approached every house with military determination. "I'm Charles Manson, in case you can't tell. He murdered a bunch of people a gazillion years ago. You can look him up on Wikipedia. They call him an *American Criminal.*"

Most people nod, amused by her forwardness. "See," she says, stepping back to form a line with Niall and Lluvia, "Manson, Mermaid, Monk. Alliteration, you know? We're the opposite of each other," she says pointing to Niall. "He's good and I'm bad. And she's—I don't know, *not real.*"

She usually garners a laugh. "How precocious," some people say. When he and Lluvia eschew offers of candy, Lluvia saying, "We'll eat some of hers," Flora counters, "Oh no you won't."

Halfway through the third block he's beat, thinking of the warmth of his bed, the blessed oblivion of sleep. He's too old for trick-or-treating, and it will take forever to complete Flora's plan.

"You're quiet tonight," Lluvia observes.

"I'm really tired. I think I should get home."

"But we just started," Flora says. "We need you."

"I have to teach tomorrow."

"I have school too."

"But you're young. I'm an old man."

"Don't be a wuss."

"I *am* a wuss and I have to go." A blip of unexpected anger flares—how annoying she is. He turns quickly, rudely, no hugs or kisses for either of them. He hops off the sidewalk to the asphalt where the pavement is smoother, and he race-walks to his car, pursued by Flora's calls: "Oh Niall, don't go!" And Lluvia's quieter echoes, "Please, Niall."

As he parks outside his building he spots someone who looks like Mateo. Dressed as a football player and walking with another younger boy, maybe his brother, dressed at Batman. Niall hurries up the walkway, eager to avoid engagement. Back inside he peels off his wet robe. It's only 7:45. He flops onto his bed in his underwear wishing he'd nabbed some candy. All he had to eat before trick-or-treating was a quick bowl of Rocio's fish soup. He's still hungry, but too lazy to seek whatever food he might have in his fridge.

Lluvia will be angry at him for leaving so abruptly. She will tell him he has disappointed Flora, as if disappointing a child is a major offense. He isn't fit for family life, for needing to be at certain places on command, for pretending to be jolly when he feels only bleak. What if he were to genuinely lose his temper at Flora and do something even more hurtful?

He finds Lluvia's number. The text he sends is not blasphemous, but nor is it one God would sanction. It is not one he himself sanctions. *I think you and I should part ways.*

They can talk later—for now he goes to bed.

23

At sunrise the sky hangs gray and bloody as a surgical patient in slow recovery. An early-morning beach jogger picks her way through candy wrappers, plastic Halloween bags, condoms, shards of broken beer bottles, syringes, mingled with the usual driftwood, stranded jellyfish, dead crabs, waterlogged kelp. She's no stranger to the detritus of this beach, but today things are worse than usual. An agate illuminated by a ray of sunlight turns out to be a melting Jolly Rancher. How she resents her regular running route being turned into a trash heap. The very air smells of excess sugar and alcohol.

A patch of black sand ahead confuses her. Oil, she suspects, though she's not aware of a recent spill. She bends to examine it and sees its black spray paint covering the sand with lines like ancient runes. Orange spray paint, too, the color of flaggers' vests. She curses the Halloween revelers and resumes her run under a dome of raucous gulls, their calls more hoarse than usual, their snippiness, she imagines, brought on by having ingested too much plastic.

She doubles back at the building that marks two and a half miles, making her run a total of five miles. She walks for a few paces, appreciating the solitude of dawn. Along the boardwalk more defacing paint grabs her attention, slashes of black on the façade of the Paramount movie theater, red on the wooden slats of the boardwalk, more black and orange on the benches where sightseers often sit and gaze out to the ocean. Someone will have to clean all this up, and the city will foot the bill. Damn these mischief makers. Don't they see that this surpasses mere playful mischief? She snaps photos, determined to make the revelers pay. On her way back down the beach she photographs the spray-painted sand too.

After her run she emails the mayor's office. *The beach and boardwalk should not be defaced like this*, she writes, and she includes the photos to justify her indignation.

The following day the local paper sounds the alarm, quoting the Mayor: *This is unacceptable behavior. Our community will not tolerate racist images defiling our public spaces. We will make every effort to track down and prosecute the perpetrators.*

The jogger examines her photos again. Racist images? She puts it together slowly. *ACS,* an acronym for Atlantic City Skins which the article mentions. And yes, the toxic symbol of the Celtic Cross.

Niall subscribes to the local paper, receiving a hard copy in his mailbox daily, because he feels it's his duty as a teacher to know about the local news. It is filled with mostly trivial stories of cat rescues and break-ins, announcements about upcoming roadwork and street closures, listings of group meetings and who is performing at the casinos. He appreciates the inclusions of daily high and low tides, and occasionally he reads letters of outrage to the editor, but mostly he skims the paper and tosses it.

The article on the front page, about the beach defacement, however, catches his attention, and he reads it from beginning to end. He has never heard of the Atlantic City Skins, a white nationalist group centered in New Jersey. The search leads him to many things he never knew. Apparently there are a handful of hate groups stationed in New Jersey, some local, some part of larger national groups. He is led to a page about the Celtic Cross, drawn in a variety of ways, which has come to express hatred in the US, though in Ireland, where it originated, it still holds religious significance. He comes across a site with page after page of more white supremacist symbols, most of which he doesn't recognize. He's sorry to see that the number eight, such a perfect even number, has also been appropriated by these hate groups too, because of H (for Hitler) being the eighth letter of the alphabet.

How can he have been oblivious to these things right in his back yard? He tucks the paper into his school bag, in case he decides to discuss the incident in class.

24

He woke to a sound at his window. Light from a pale moon limned wavering shadows, ghoulish shapes. *A cow has escaped,* he thought, and he listened for the clopping of hooves before the face at the window became human. Bearded. Eyes coruscating dark wells. He sat up, suppressing a gasp.

The window reverted to its still, monochrome gray. He waited. Watched. Was there anyone else with glittering eyes like that, stuck in their depths like prune stones?

It could have been a dream. Yet, he was sure he'd seen what he'd seen.

The mind plays tricks, he told himself, lying back down, wondering what the Abbot would say, knowing he wouldn't tell the Abbot, whose loyalties were clear.

The next night a flock of honking Canada geese awakened him. He opened his eyes on impenetrable darkness, a cloudy winter night, no moonlight to help him see. It was cold, the scent of imminent snow tingeing the air. Against that cold the heat of a proximate body was unmistakable. It reached him as a soundless wind, wave after wave brushing his cheek.

"Hello?" he said into the darkness. His ears scraped the room's contours for the creak of bones, a telltale intake of breath. If someone were in here with him there would have to be some sound—but there was no sound.

An ache accompanied his widening irises, and the unyielding blackness gave way to a lighter black, then a porous gray which exposed a robed silhouette, its features blotted. He lay there, eyes unblinking, fixated, testing his senses and mind, his heartbeat drowning out every other noise, but for the faintest of crackling. Was the heat he felt his own feverishness? He could have turned on the light or called out, but he couldn't bring himself to do either. If it were Brother Thomas—and who else could it be—what would he say? What *could* he say? He closed his eyes, afraid he was going crazy, and after a minute he turned from his back to his belly, thrashing loudly as he did so, giving the intruder a chance to exit with dignity, incognito.

First, it was once a week. Then, every other night. Eventually the intrusions occurred nightly. Never knowing exactly when they would happen, he couldn't fall asleep. At some point he stopped keeping track of the hours—he would hear the door handle turning, the quiet soughing of human movement. If his eyes were open, he would see the man's robed figure silhouetted by a spray of light from the corridor. Mostly he kept his eyes closed, his ears transcribing pictures from sounds. The click of the closing door. Darkness. Slippers across floorboards. The hovering by the bed for a moment which was a sound in itself: body swaying, the mingling of breath and air. The intensity of the intruder's presence oozed past Niall's closed lids with the venom of a bad dream.

Then, the large body would descend in deliberate collapse to the floor, bones knocking floorboards, a sigh, a grunt. Stretching, groaning, followed by the final settling and a long exhale. As if to say: *Here I am stretched out on your floor. This is the self-flagellation I endure for you.*

Neither one of them slept. Countless insomniac nights passed this way, Thomas on the floor, both of them listening and exchanging breath, only pretending to sleep. Niall had been at the monastery for almost five years by then—why was this escalation of torture happening now?

Niall spent his days bleary-eyed, confused, often nodding off in the chapel, during devotions and chanting, during his studies. He was fearful and enraged, but also confused. Brother Thomas's earlier provocations had been more understandable—he was clearly jealous of Niall's friendship with Francis—but if these middle-of-the-night intrusions were a form of proposition, why was Thomas being so roundabout? He was much bigger than Niall. If he wanted sex he could take Niall by force. The restraint made no sense, and it told Niall that these visitations were the actions of a complicated, deeply disturbed man.

One night, after three weeks of these visits in which neither of them had said a word, Niall trying with all his might to pretend nothing out of the ordinary was happening, gruff whispered words rose from the floor: "Do me."

Niall feigned sleep, deepening and elongating his breath.

"I know you heard me. Take me."

A few more long breaths before Niall gave in. "I'm not that way."

"How do you know?"

"I know."

"I could take you if I chose to. I've done it before."

"I'm sure you have, but please don't."

The fraught air seemed to buzz. Niall's terror cut off his breath. Brother Thomas rose from the floor. If Niall kept his eyes closed it wouldn't happen. He could feel Thomas close to the bed, studying him, a furnace of heat and intention. Thomas sat, his weight tilting the mattress. Niall couldn't find breath to speak. A hard wallop landed on his hip bone.

"Stop being so full of yourself," Thomas said. "You're young, but there are plenty of other better men than you. I'm too old for this." As he rose, the mattress sprang back. The door opened, closed. Quiet. Niall opened his eyes, still holding his breath.

The next night Thomas did not come but, not knowing what to expect, Niall did not sleep. There was no visitation the following night. Or the night after that. It took a month for Niall to begin to sleep again, but only in short snatches of twenty or thirty minutes, before he would jerk awake, alert to the slightest of sounds.

The insomnia was ruining him for anything else. In the kitchen, stirring the cheese curds, he scalded his hand. When milking, he irritated one of the cows who stepped on his toes and bruised them badly. He watered the ficus tree in the atrium until its pot overflowed. He dropped his hymnal as he was singing. He stumbled along the pathways as if drunk, spilled a full can of blue paint in the dining room.

The Abbot drew him aside in the empty chapel after morning prayers. He spoke more sharply than usual. "You're becoming inattentive and sloppy. What has happened to your discipline?"

It was still dark out, the chapel dim. The Abbot's face was dipped in shadow, eradicating his kind eyes, so there was nothing to counteract the seemingly malign intent borne by his words. Niall saw the end coming. He would be asked to leave for insubordination. Or insufficient devotion. *Go ahead, kick me out,* he thought. "I'll do better," he said.

A month passed without visits from Thomas, but Niall remained sleepless, desperate for relief. He requested an urgent meeting with the Abbot—he knew the Abbot's sympathies lay with Thomas, but it seemed as if it was the Abbot's job to help resolve this problem, this internecine struggle.

The Abbot acquiesced to a meeting, but it would have to be brief—a few minutes only—as he was due to meet with someone else off campus. It was after the evening meal, late April. It was still light but, standing in the Abbot's office, he was aware of light and time and his own credibility slipping away.

"It isn't my fault," he blurted. Hearing how defensive he sounded, he drew breath and began again. "Thomas has been coming into my room in the middle of the night unannounced, wanting . . ." He could not bring himself to say the word, to impugn the Abbot's nephew.

"Yes? Go on,"

"You know . . . I never know when he's going to come in and it keeps me awake."

"What are you telling me? Get to the point. I have to leave soon. You're saying you don't want Brother Thomas visiting you?"

"Yes."

"Have you told him this?"

"Yes, yes. Several times. But he doesn't listen. And I thought if you said something, being his uncle, it would have more impact on him."

The Abbot's entire bearing changed. "What do you want me to do?"

Niall could feel himself shrinking. "Can't you get him to stop?"

"Brother Anselm, are you a grownup or are you not? You have to stand up for yourself. It is not my job to resolve this."

Niall drooped further. "But I . . ."

"I have to go. Ask for God's help. You'll do fine."

They left the office together, neither of them having sat down to make it a real meeting. The Abbot paused to lock his office door. Niall stood at the Abbot's back, inches away. Pedestals on both sides of the door held urns displaying large Easter lilies, white and fragrant, their protuberant stamens beginning to shed pollen.

"Sex," Niall whispered. "He's been asking for sex."

The Abbot turned and traversed the lobby at his usual moderate pace.

Niall felt trapped now, truly without recourse. Two miles from the buildings, far beyond everyone's earshot, he spilled everything to Brother Francis on one of their walks. Brother Francis already knew things were going wrong, and he'd been waiting for Niall to talk.

Niall collapsed on a stone wall by the path and broke down.

Francis sat beside him. "He's unpredictable, maybe bipolar, I don't know. At any rate, he doesn't belong here. I hoped for a while that the Abbot would see that and find another place for him, but I don't think that will happen. We could go above the Abbot's head, but, oh dear. I just don't know." He sighed and stroked Niall's back. "I can't stand to see him poisoning things for you. Perhaps I can speak to him?"

"Would you?"

"I'll try."

True to his word one day Francis drew Thomas aside in the corner of the cow barn after milking when they were the only two there. He spoke as gently as he could. "Please back off," he said, placing a steadying hand on Thomas's shoulder. "Brother Anselm has been clear with you, hasn't he?"

Thomas recoiled, glared at Francis. "Who do you think you are? Let the bastard speak for himself," he growled and stalked away.

Francis reported this to Niall with tremors of sorrow in his voice, his eyes, his whole demeanor. "This shouldn't be happening. Here of all places. Don't let it break you."

They stared at each other, shook their heads, embraced.

With nothing resolved, his insomnia persisted. A choice was imminent. One night, during a sleepless stretch, he sat up, reached in the dark for his water glass and gulped. He gagged, spat, retched onto his lap, purging an acid vileness.

He switched on the lamp, stared at the mess he'd made of himself. The water glass evinced a strange color. He held it up to the light, sniffed. It wasn't water—it was urine.

25

Laboring in the fields, the dank barns, the steamy kitchen, the men clothed in their woolen robes sweated, fluid streaming down their necks and foreheads and backs and torsos, drying at night into an invisible crust of salt until they bathed on the third day, so most often they smelled gamey, each emitting different chemical compounds according to their DNA and their diet (though everyone's diet was basically the same). Niall's sense of smell sharpened, so he could identify many of the men by their body odors. Brother Gregory, in his eighties and succumbing to dementia, gave off the plaque-y smell of unbrushed teeth and over-ripe cheese. It seemed to presage imminent death, but he still performed his labors with good humor alongside the other brothers, albeit a little more slowly and with supervision. Simon, in his sixties, smelled like pipe tobacco so strongly Niall wondered if he was a secret smoker, but over time Niall decided it was simply Simon's makeup. Martin reminded Niall of a pond in the woods, somewhat fresh, somewhat algal; Stephen exuded the scent of a certain kind of pollen Niall had smelled before, remarkably similar to the scent of semen. The Abbot gave off a smell that was not entirely natural. A man-made musky, male perfume, an unexpected vanity for him to indulge in. Curiously, Thomas's scent was more pleasing than most, like some plant Niall had no name for, green and glowing.

Niall remembers his formerly sharp sense of smell when he holds the conferences with his students. He thought this enhanced ability was peculiar to his time in the monastery, but now he sees he was mistaken. Thrust into close physical proximity with his students when they sit in the plastic orange chair a foot from his desk, he notices all kinds of things he hasn't registered before. He counts Jayden's fifteen ear and nose piercings, even his tongue is pierced. He sees the tattoo on the inside of Rania's wrist that says *LIVE*, the rose tattoo on Shannel's collarbone, the dark brown freckles bridging Camilla's pale nose. And he smells them too, hormone-rich and cologne-scented, different from the monks, but equally as pungent due to the churning hormones of their youth, their high-octane lives. It's hard not to attribute some of their smells to active sex lives, though he tries to suppress this embarrassing thought and keep the focus on their papers.

He has only seven minutes with each student. He has to be strict with the time to get through them all in the days he has allotted. Having never written lengthy research papers before, they all need help. Some of them have taken notes on their topics, but no one has made much progress except Rania, who is writing about Muslims during Jim Crow and has already made a detailed outline.

It's Colton's turn. Niall busies himself with nonessential papers on his desk while Colton settles into the chair. Even without looking at him Niall feels the palpable presence of his muscularity making a statement alongside his aggressive male cologne. Beside Colton, Niall feels slight and feeble, haphazardly groomed, the same attributes that made him generally overlooked as a child.

Colton places a notebook on the desk with a ceremonial arc of his arm and leans forward, uncharacteristically eager, opening the notebook and ironing the page flat with his palm. Apparently he is proud.

"I've done a lot," he says. "You know, research."

"Great!" Niall says. He stares at the page Colton has opened to.

There are columns of words written in the indecipherable scrawl of a child. A learning disability, Niall remembers Colton's mother saying, dyslexia. A pang of sympathy passes through him. "Good for you, Colton. Tell me about it."

"So, the boardwalk thing, right, on Halloween? I'm gonna write about, you know, why some people think white people are smarter than other people."

Niall nods only because no other response comes to him. He feels stupid, aphasic. *White people.* Colton wants to write about *white people*?

"Say more," Niall says.

"You know, all the white people who want the immigrants and colored people out."

"Colored people?"

"People of color. Whatever. The point is so many people think those people don't belong here, and I wanna write about that. Why it is, you know? What makes them think that?"

"*Those people.* You mean the black and brown people?"

"Yeah, them."

"Think about the words you use, Colton. The words you choose convey a lot."

"Why are you always nit-picking with me when you know what I mean?"

"I don't actually know what you mean. I need to clarify that you don't believe that—that immigrants and people of color don't belong here?"

Colton slaps his forehead. "There you go again, assuming the worst about me."

"I'm just trying to understand."

Colton's head swivels out to the other students. Most are bent over their papers, but Mason is watching them, and he and Colton shake their heads in solidarity. Some of the other students look up, corralled by the jiggling synapses of Colton's energy. Turning back to Niall, Colton's entire body is tense with fury, and Niall feels a matching fury mounting in himself.

"Look, Colton, this is an ambitious topic. We need more time to discuss it. Can you come back today after school?"

Colton slaps his notebook closed and scrapes back his chair. Niall is suddenly scared of him, equally scared of himself.

After school Colton stands at the classroom door looking no more tame than earlier. His toned body. The backward black cap. His blond-brown hair, corralled in a ponytail. Brown eyes set off by darker brown eyebrows. He would be attractive were it not for his attitude.

"I can't stay long, I have practice."

"Ten minutes. I'll write you a note explaining why you're late. Come in."

Colton strolls in and perches on the edge of one of the tables closest to the door, a tentative posture. Niall perches at the edge of his desk.

"Can't you see I'm trying?"

"I see that. Tell me more about your project."

Sighing, Colton opens his notebook and stares down at the page. Silence. Ten, fifteen, twenty seconds. He brings out his phone, the same phone with the picture of Niall and Trinity laughing. Niall has to exert supreme restraint to keep from grabbing it.

"Okay—so there were things on the boardwalk the cops didn't see. See here." He holds his phone out, not moving from his perch, so Niall has to move toward him to see it. "Look closely—see, 88s everywhere." He brings up photos of the corners of the building's façade, the back of a bench, a parked car, and zooms in to splashes of black spray paint. 8s, Celtic Crosses, and various other symbols Niall vaguely recognizes from his own Googling.

Colton restores his phone to his pocket. "So, the thing is, it wasn't just the Skins. You've got people here from the Creativity

Movement. You've got the Shamrock, that's for the Aryan Brotherhood."

Niall nods.

"It was a lot of different groups, I think. I'm gonna track them down and interview them and ask what they think they're doing. How they got involved in this shit, and how are they gonna bring about the world they imagine? And why would it be better? You know, all that stuff."

"You don't think it might be difficult to get to them? Even dangerous? They might not be willing to talk to you. Especially if the police are after them."

Colton shrugs. "I know a few people." Colton hooks Niall's gaze, holds it fast for several beats during which Niall's gut seizes.

Niall stands to get control of himself. Cut the kid a break. Just because he *knows a few people* doesn't mean . . . Niall walks around behind his desk. "Okay, Colton, you're good to go now."

But Colton lingers, butt still welded to the edge of the table, wagging his foot. "Wait—you haven't said—I mean, do you think it's, like, a good project? Could I get an A?"

Niall hesitates. "If you can pull it off it could be good."

"Just good?"

"Okay, very good. Just do the work and we'll see."

Appearing satisfied, Colton stands. "My mom will be happy to hear that."

"One more thing," Niall says. "Would you please delete the photo of me and Ms. White?"

Colton salutes. "Sure, boss, whatever you say."

Niall studies Colton's face to find the locus of his sarcasm. The lips? The eyes? The forward thrust of his hips? *Trust the boy.*

After Colton leaves Niall locks his classroom door and, overcome with exhaustion, he lies on the floor against the wall, out of view of anyone peering in from the hallway. He welcomes the penance of the cold linoleum, a harsh spray of air blowing out from the heating vent a few feet away, drying his eyes but beginning to calm him. He can't penetrate Colton's intentions. How does he know these unsavory people he claims to know? Niall wishes he could talk to Lluvia and find out what she thinks. She has always brought him perspective and helped him relax, just like Abbot Jerome sometimes did. But since Halloween they haven't talked, though he's been meaning to reach out. So abruptly, it would be opportunistic and shameful to get in touch with her now. She wouldn't refuse him, being the good human being she is, but he would feel guilty. He wonders if she, a brown person, would know about the groups Colton was referring to. Trinity certainly does, dialed in as she is.

He's acutely aware of being unfit for his job. He has too many cultural deficits, too soft a voice, too much of a tendency towards anger. But how can he possibly quit yet another enterprise?

He'd like to talk to Trinity too, but he hasn't seen her since the Vaseline incident earlier in the week, and he feels too naïve, too *white*, too consumed by whether the Vaseline attack was prompted by his association with Trinity and the rumors of their intimacy.

As if he has summoned her, she texts. *Manhattan tomorrow? We'll hit the gallery, have some coffee. Talk where no one will see us. I'll pick you up at 10. Send your address.*

Manhattan terrifies him. Since he has moved to New Jersey he hasn't been there at all. But with Trinity as his guide it might not be so bad. A talented college friend of hers is having an exhibition, and she promises it will be good. He texts her back with his address and a thumbs up. He was headed for a long, solitary, unscheduled weekend—it's good to have a plan.

He continues to lie on the floor, unable to galvanize himself to move. The school is quieter than he ever remembers the monastery being. He thinks of Thomas lying on his wooden floor all night, filled with desire, confusion, envy, hatred. On his best days Niall understands Thomas as a sad man. On his worst days he sees Thomas as a conduit and amplifier for the worst parts of himself.

Niall opens his eyes on the bright light of a sunny beach. An eye doctor's headlamp? He closes them quickly.

"Hey man, are you okay?"

Opening his eyes again, Niall sees it's Pete standing over him. "I fell asleep." He remembers the wisp of a dream—Buttercup was getting feisty and was stomping on his feet as he was tried to skitter out of her way. He needs to get up, but he's too weak. He grabs the leg of a nearby table and pulls himself to sitting.

"What happened?" Pete asks. "Shall I call for help?"

"Oh no, I'm fine. Just tired. A long week."

Pete helps him to stand, gives him a dubious assessing look. "Maybe you should get yourself to a doctor."

"I'm fine, really." He shrugs off Pete's consoling hand and gathers his bag and coat from his desk. "Have a good evening, Pete."

"You take care. Have a good weekend."

Only when he is halfway down the dark corridor does he remember he should have asked Pete about the Vaseline in Trinity's room, see what Pete thinks happened. He can't bring himself to go back.

It's already dark. The thought of the weekend defeats him. Too much unscheduled time for his thoughts to go awry. In the difficult days of middle school his mother used to ask him what he looked forward to. Even a small thing would help, she said, such as what he would have for lunch; it could sustain him through the bad hours. He made lists of small things that pleased him: watching a movie with Adam, the younger boy who lived across the street and looked up to him; the biology class where they would be dissecting frogs; sitting behind Rachel Ludlow in English class and savoring the way wisps of hair on her neck were blown by the heating system like small fairies.

He tries to employ his mother's technique now. He remembers the plan he made with Trinity to go into Manhattan. That will help distract him, and it will be good to talk. And maybe he'll indulge in a movie one night, if there's anything good to see.

He parks under a streetlight across from his building, goes to fetch his bag from the trunk. The streetlight illuminates the dirt and dust on his rear windshield—he's never seen the point of keeping a car clean for it to become dirty as soon as it's driven again. Marks on the glass come into focus, registering like bullets. *H8, H8, H8.* He doubts what he sees, moves to a different angle. But nothing changes.

He grabs his bag and hurries across the street. Behind him someone opens a car door, slams it. Footsteps follow him. He begins to sprint, the footsteps behind him light but quick. At the building's entrance he fumbles with his key, drops it, bends to retrieve it. Lluvia beats him to it. He lets out a cry and collapses into her. Her curls tickle his face. He weeps with relief.

They go inside. The place smells of stale coffee; he remembers the pot of days-old mac-and-cheese he left on the stove.

"What could I do? You weren't answering my texts," she says. He can't defend himself. The failure is his, not hers. He's glad she's here, her familiar face, her body leaning into him, sprinkling him with its floral scent. He tries to control his trembling; they're inside now, safe. But he's still afraid. Someone must be after him.

She helps him with his coat, ushers him to the bedroom as if he's one of her disabled patients. Perched on the edge of the bed he starts to speak. He tells her about Colton's project, the Vaseline on Trinity's floor, the marks on his windshield. Does she know what H8 means? Yes, she does. Everything is connected, he says, an ominous whole. The world is a terrible place.

"But it's what we've got—so we enjoy the good parts."

"But—"

She hushes him, draws back the quilt, unbuttons, unzips, shucks his clothing, a deft expert. She pushes him down on the mattress, and he stops resisting her and shuts up, lying on his back, watching her undress.

Naked, she pauses beside the bed, displaying herself, not seductively but announcing herself: *Here I am.* Her astonishing body, a persuasion, a pleasure beyond heaven that he has renounced. He looks away as she slips under the covers, feeling unentitled to her body, to everything lovely about her that makes the world a better place.

"Are you angry at me?" he asks. "Most people would be furious."

"Yes, of course. But I don't think you mean it."

He stares at the ceiling, considering her claim. He can't understand why she's so resistant, so keen on giving him another chance. He knows himself reasonably well, knows things about himself she has no idea about.

"Flora doesn't want me to let you go either. She likes you. She's wise, wiser than I am. You know how kids are."

He has no idea how kids are, his only experience his own childhood long ago. He remembers his flash of annoyance at Flora when he left them on Halloween. But she likes him anyway?

"I want to take you to Puerto Rico, and show you where I grew up. We'll walk on the beach and swim and you'll relax. We'll bring back some of that island feeling."

He adjusts the pillow to alleviate a crick in his neck. Isn't Puerto Rico a mess now from all the recent hurricanes?

"Do you think you'll still be teaching six years from now? Flora will be in college then, and I'll be free to go anywhere."

These plans of hers. A future all mapped out. Marriage. Home ownership. Trips to Puerto Rico. All he sees is the rot in the world—someone out to get him and Trinity. "Let's talk in the morning. I'm exhausted."

"Promise you'll talk?" she says, "You won't clam up on me?" She squeezes her eyes as if they're clamshells and, laughing, kisses his shoulder, his forehead, his chest, his lips.

"Promise." He pats her thigh and rolls over.

He sleeps until 9:30, more exhausted than he knew. He hears Lluvia in the kitchen, and within minutes, sensing he's awake, she brings him a mugful of coffee and holding one for herself. Casting off her blouse, she climbs back into bed, snuggling up beside him.

"Now you can say whatever you want. You don't really think someone is after you, do you?"

"I do. Maybe."

"Well, we should find out who it is and report them."

"Easier said than done."

"Tell me how you're much too terrible to be with me, and I'll tell you once again how wrong you are." She laughs quietly, so sure of her value and his.

With the first sip of coffee, he remembers his date with Trinity. He needs to cancel and bring full attention to this conversation with Lluvia. He lays his mug on the bedside table and reaches for his phone. As if someone has seen him, a text comes through. *I'm downstairs. Sorry I'm early. Take your time.*

26

The quiet was deeper than usual. A white sky all the way to the horizon. Something unreachable lurked behind it. Something forbidden.

He was crossing a line he'd never crossed before. As a child tried so hard to be good, he'd always recoiled at the merest suggestion he might be bad. He wasn't anything like Kevin Dineen or Ron Pugliese, bullies and fighters, always being punished. There were only a few times his mother had made him feel he had disappointed her, not many. She had even accepted his temper tantrums as part of normal development. But once he took Liam's electronic keyboard, a Christmas present. He only meant to borrow it for a few minutes while Liam was out, but he spilled his orange juice over it so all the keys stuck, and it had to be taken in for repair. *You know better,* his mother said. And she was right.

Why, my son? Abbot Jerome would ask now. God himself would be horrified. But if the Abbot had drunk another man's urine, wouldn't he feel driven to do something? Niall, propelled by the drumbeat of indignation and the lingering repugnant taste in his mouth, pushed away thoughts of a horrified God. He turned the handle, stepped inside, closed the door quietly behind him. Brother Thomas was gone for the afternoon on procurement detail. The other brothers were at work around the grounds and buildings. Niall was shirking his own assignment in the kitchen. Someone would come looking for him, but not yet.

He stood still in amazement. The dazzle of spaciousness. Multiples windows. Cherry woodwork. Plush wine-colored carpeting. A fireplace with two amethyst-velvet easy chairs arranged in front of it. A separate sleeping area with a king bed, crimson quilt, matching shams. By one window a study with a large oak desk, computer, small speakers, a bookshelf with *The Solace of Poetry* on the top shelf. A kitchen area with sink and stove, refrigerator stocked with bread, cheeses, luncheon meats, milk and bottled water, chocolate and coffee ice cream in the freezer. One cupboard with plates and glassware, another with coffee and tea, honey and sugar, bottles of wine and vodka and gin and whiskey. An adjoining private bathroom with shower stall, crimson towels and washcloths, vetiver-scented soap, Thomas's smell. A closet of civilian clothing—trousers, silk shirts, leather jackets, cashmere sweaters.

Niall wandered around opening cupboards and closets, trailing his hands over everything in stunned disbelief. Did the other brothers know of this luxurious enclave, this duplicity, this flouting of the life of poverty? Francis had never mentioned it—maybe he didn't know. And why wasn't the room locked? Apparently Thomas felt no need to hide.

Footsteps outside. Someone coming to find him? He held his breath until the footsteps receded then slipped back into the empty corridor, dizzied by the quiet.

27

The painting's iridescent green wax background shimmers under the gallery's spotlight. A black tree branch, gnarled, witchy. Perched on it a large black bird—a crow? a magpie? a raven?—stares into the painting's distance at a flock of its own kind which is becoming tiny and formless as it's devoured by the white of sky. The canvas, huge and placed at the center of a white wall, calls out to be noticed.

Trinity stands before it, entranced, ignoring what Niall has just told her about the H8s on his rear window and about Colton's photograph of the two of them. She took this information in without saying much, shrugging, implying he was overreacting. But these things mean something, don't they? He doesn't understand why she isn't more upset.

"You're giving him too much power," she told him. "Forget about Colton—he's a mosquito. If he thinks we're a couple, let him think that. I don't care—you're a good guy."

"But he knows these terrible people. Isn't that something to be worried about?"

"Yeah, we'll keep an eye on him. But it's premature to point the finger. If you're wrong about him, it would be trouble."

"And the H8s—what am I supposed to think about that? You don't think that's Colton's work?"

"People who do that are everywhere. Maybe not at your perfect little monastery, but the rest of the world is filled with them. You've got to ignore them so they don't get the upper hand."

She drifts off to join the painter and his fans, former classmates, all black. He feels like an outsider and can't bring himself to join them. He wonders if she's right to not worry. He can't focus on the art, everything he looks at is overlaid with the crumpled look of Lluvia's face when he departed. Why did he leave? He doesn't understand himself. He's an asshole.

The sacred hush of the gallery soothes him somewhat, the unexpected alcoves and inviting pockets of light, the whispers of the other patrons. He has missed this sense of collective respect that asks for silence.

Later, in a noisy Chelsea café, he admires the leaf etched into the foam of his cappuccino. On the plate beside his coffee is a turkey, cheese, and pesto panini, garnished with a display of parsley, avocado slices, and pomegranate seeds. He can't remember the last time he ate such elegant-looking food. It's almost as stunning as the artwork. He tries to put his worries aside and appreciate, at least for this day, the sheath of anonymity the city confers on him—he could vanish here so no one would be able to find him.

"I should come here more often," he says. "It's so close." But even as he says this he knows he won't come here on his own. "Shit," he says, overcome again by a memory of Lluvia's crestfallen face. "I shouldn't have left Lluvia. I'm such an asshole."

"Ease up. You'll get over it, and so will she. I promise. That's how breakups go. You just have to ride it out." She looks at him and chuckles, appalled yet again by his naiveté. "You're such a worrywart."

They walk around the West Village and down to the Lower East Side, dipping into shops and bookstores that interest Trinity. Niall follows willingly, with no purpose of his own but to calm himself. The sun emerges in the late afternoon, painting the west-facing facades pink and making faces glow. As they descend to the PATH train, he finds himself reluctant to leave the city. He wants to hold onto the anonymity, step into the city at night and delve deeper into its secrets. The things he faces back in New Jersey are complicated, guilt-inducing, frightening. There are plenty of better men out there for Lluvia, men who are ready to take on the role of husband, devoted father and son-in-law. As for Colton, maybe Trinity is right—maybe he should try to think less about Colton.

Trinity drops him off at home. He eats a banana and a Clif bar, and goes to bed.

28

In the middle of Niall's worst troubles with Thomas, Niall welcomed being assigned to procurement detail with Brother Francis. It was a chance to leave the monastery to drive together to town for groceries and supplies. It was a rural town of fifteen hundred people, most of its businesses catering to small farmers. The task took the better part of the afternoon, stopping at the feed store, the hardware store, the supermarket, occasionally going to the next town for stationery supplies. As a weekly chore it might have been drudgery, but Niall was assigned to the job only every few months, and he always welcomed the opportunity to set aside an afternoon of study to ride in the van, savor the beauty of the surrounding farmland, glance at newspapers, chat with store clerks, reminding himself of what he'd forsaken. It was an extra pleasure to make the trip with Francis, a consummate storyteller, always in high spirits. And that day it was especially appealing as a way of getting away from Thomas.

They bought in bulk—rice and beans, grains for the livestock, extra milk for cheese-making to augment their own supply—and their orders were placed ahead of time so the purchases were usually waiting for them on the loading dock or at the front of the store. They would heft the weighty bags and boxes into the van, exertion that invariably resulted in sore muscles the next day, making Niall realize his daily schedule of study and prayer and worship was not benefiting his body.

Niall sometimes did the driving himself, but with Francis he was always a passenger and that day, exhausted from so many sleepless nights, he sat back and stared out at the browning pastures, autumn beginning to redden the maple leaves, some of the late crops, mostly squash and pumpkins, waiting to be harvested, but most of the fields already plowed over and lying fallow, ready for winter.

"Urine, Francis. Urine! Who would do that? Can you believe it?"

"Sadly, I can."

"So I went into his room. I didn't care if I was trespassing. It wasn't locked. Have you seen it?"

"No. But I've heard the rumors. He isn't living in poverty, I understand."

"My god, it's palatial. Beautiful, of course, but disgusting."

"Part of his package, I guess."

"Why does he have *a package?* What is he? A CEO? A president? A pope? It's not right."

"No, it's not right."

They fall into silence.

"Why doesn't it make you mad?"

"There are so many things in this world that aren't right, and we can't fix them. If we let them all enrage us, we'd be stuck there, mad all the time, right?"

"But right here, under our own roof!"

"Don't waste your anger, Anselm, on something we can't fix."

"I know you're right, but . . ."

"The bile isn't good for you. I know firsthand. I lived for so many years spewing out the bad black bile of envy and victimhood. I was never getting what I thought I deserved. I fear all that bile has left its mark. I feel old these days."

"You're not old."

"Old enough." Francis laughed. "Look at my gut and my double chin. Everything is sagging and breaking down. But I'm not worried. I think there might be some perks to being old. You're going to be wheeling me around in a wheelchair soon, and I won't have to lift a finger. Finally, the life of Riley."

"Not soon, Francis. That's a long way off. And the way things are going, I'll probably get there first."

At Mack's Feedstore the employees were genial and helpful, having worked with the brothers for over fifty years, and they sent out two of their burliest workers, Shep and Rip, to hurl the fifty-pound bags of feed into the back of the van. When they were done the men slapped Niall and Francis's backs as if they were all kinsmen, a gesture that made Niall irrationally happy.

At the supermarket Francis bought jumbo packs of fun-size Milky Ways and Mars bars and peanut butter cups, glancing at Niall, knowing his secret was safe. They opened the bags immediately and stuffed their mouths. Having forgotten the wheelbarrow to transport the hundred gallons of milk, they had to make twenty-five trips in and out of the store, each of them carrying two gallons at a time. Terrible inefficiency, but nothing about their lives was organized around efficiency.

It was a hot, dusty day, too hot for their wool robes, but Niall had become used to such discomfort by then and scarcely noticed the rivulets of sweat breaking paths down his back and legs. He hoisted a bag of dried red beans over his shoulder as if it were a cowl, feeling like an authentic member of the working class. A thud behind him. Francis had gone down, his slack torso splayed across a bag of rice, his face skyward. Niall dropped his beans, sped to Francis and laid an ear over his heart. A beat was present, but Francis was unconscious. Niall moved as quickly as he could, summoning help, trying not to panic.

29

Home from Manhattan, Niall lies on his couch and prepares himself to call Lluvia. He has no idea what he'll say. The trip to the city swims in his mind along with the picture of the new life it spawned: blissful anonymity amidst the chaos, no attachments, no obligations. If Lluvia were to visit his mind and see this escape fantasy of his, she would know it's in her best interest to flee from him.

He picks up the phone, ready to wing it, his heart thumping so hard he's afraid she might hear it. He sees a voicemail message from her, sent that morning. *What a coward you are.* And she weeps.

The outlines for the research papers of his fifth period class are due on Monday. He situates himself at his desk, awaiting their arrival, his mood glum, his expectations glummer. It's possible they've blown him off entirely and not done any work. Jayden is the first to enter, body and mouth whizzing.

"I'm dropping knowledge here, Mr. O." He lays his backpack on Niall's desk and withdraws a stack of paper-clipped pages.

"Good for you!"

A deluge follows. "I didn't sleep the whole weekend," Dominic declares, tossing his pages at Niall. "I did good. That shit is on point, mister."

Every last one of them has something to give him. Tiffany, Aliyah,

Camilla, Rania, Anthony, Roman, Mateo, Shannel. Everyone, even the slackers. They gather around his desk, requesting paper clips and staplers, showing off the number of pages they've generated, announcing the topics they're covering: Carpetbaggers; Amendments Thirteen, Fourteen, and Fifteen; Johnson's Impeachment; the Compromise of 1877. Rania and Camilla have encased their work in colored plastic binders.

"You wanted an argument, Mr. O'Malley," Rania says gleefully, "I gave you a good argument."

Colton, sitting at his usual table, rises suddenly and joins the fray around Niall's desk. He slips a binder under the pile of accruing papers and, suppressing a grin, saunters back to his desk.

Everyone's pride in their work is such a surprise it lifts Niall's spirits a little. He finds himself tearing up. He wants to reward them.

"Would you like to dance now?"

"You're kidding?" Jayden says.

"No."

"That's what's up."

They dance for the rest of the period, Jayden taking charge as the deejay, playing music from his phone.

"Not too loud," Niall warns, "or they'll shut us down."

Niall sits on his desk watching, struck by how each of them has a distinct personal style, a hidden personality emerging. He almost thinks he should take notes so he can remember what their bodies seem to be telling him.

"Come on, oldhead. Let's see your moves," Jayden calls.

"Yeah, Mr. O. Get down with us," Rania echoes.

"*Ven*, mister, *a bailar!*"

Several other students join in. *Come on! Don't be a wimp! Let's see you boogie.*

Jayden grabs Niall's hand and tugs until Niall relents and stands and shakes his arms and head a little, trying to find the beat. He would imitate them if he could, but most of them are doing things much too quick and complicated for him to replicate, isolating limbs at the joints as if they're snap-on parts.

"Hips, dude. Move your hips!" Jayden directs.

He tries to emulate Jayden, making a mess of it, a little embarrassed, but enjoying himself nonetheless.

At the end of the period they vanish as quickly as they came, hailing him as they speed out the door. A moment that will last in his memory has come and gone for them. Only Colton remains, standing next to Niall's desk and shuffling through the stack of papers to find his own. He places it in Niall's hands. It's impressively thick, and neatly presented in a red binder.

"Tell me what you think."

"I need to read it first."

"So read it."

"Now isn't the time."

"Just have a quick look."

Niall opens the report cover. There is a Table of Contents listing four sections and a summary: 1) *The History of White Supremacy in America (an overview)* 2) *Active White Supremacist Groups in New Jersey* 3) *White Supremacist Symbols and Their Meaning* 4) *Interviews* 5) *Summary.*

"Impressive."

"Damn good, isn't it? I did a ton of work."

"Good for you."

"So read it, will you?"

"Of course I will, but not now."

"Why not—you have a free period, don't you?"

There are twenty pages, neatly typed. "Did someone help you with this?" Niall regrets his words as soon as they're out of his mouth.

"No, the dummy did it himself."

Colton's body is a hot wall between Niall and the classroom

door. It seems to vibrate with intention. No wonder he wins his wrestling matches. Niall is trapped. The only way to get free is to tell Colton he has an excellent outline that will make an A paper.

Twenty pages is far more than the assignment required. Niall flips through them, spot reading. The Table of Contents summarizes each section briefly. The third section includes a lengthy list of symbols printed from the internet, each one annotated. When he gets to the final section, the interviews, he reads more slowly. The names have been changed to protect privacy, Colton writes.

> Cindy: *You've seen the studies, right? They don't do good in school. They're always behind because they don't have the brain power. Their brains are smaller than ours. Without the brain power you might as well be an animal.*

> Dick: *Thing is, we were here first, and then they come and want to take our shit. It's wrong, just wrong. I don't know, I just don't like being around them. They smell funny. And the way they roll their eyes? It's freaky. And the Jews— they gotta get out too. Stop trying to control everything.*

> Twig: *You ever look at them closely? They've got these white patches. Their faces are really dark but then you see their palms and the soles of their feet and they're white. Like they've been painted, you know, everywhere but their feet and hands. Like they have something to hide, you know?*

Niall closes the binder, his hands shaking. "People actually said these things to you? Real people?"

"Of course they're real people. I told you—"

"Okay. I need to get moving." Niall places Colton's paper on top of the stack and puts them all in his bag.

"So?" Colton says.

"Good. You did the work."

"*Good*, that's all? I did twenty interviews, you know. It took a shitload of time."

"I'm sure it did. I look forward to reading more. But right now I have other things to attend to."

"Why are you always like this?"

"Like what?"

"You won't talk to me, even when I try."

"I'll talk to you, Colton, but not now. I have other classes to teach."

"Yeah, right." Colton swivels and heads for the door in his usual unhurried, *don't-fuck-with-me* swagger. As soon as he's gone, Niall locks the door.

Minutes later he's on the move. Sixth period has begun and the hallway is empty. He hurries to Johnson's office, hoping he's free. He didn't expect to find three people ahead of him: a student; one of the coaches; and the art teacher, Patsy. He takes the only remaining chair next to Patsy, who he worked with on lunchroom supervision. She's tougher than her appearance would lead one to believe.

"Johnson's a popular guy," Niall remarks.

"Oh, he is," Patsy says. "Don't you love him? You wouldn't know but the last principal was an a-hole, pardon my French. Really stingy. But Johnson gives me everything I ask for. My classroom is finally well-supplied."

"That's good to know."

"He certainly knows where to go for money. You're history, right? What're you asking for?"

"Oh, it's another matter—about a student."

"Oh, I'm sorry."

How does she know to be sorry? But of course one doesn't go to the principal about a student if there isn't a problem.

It takes more than half an hour before Niall gets into Johnson's office. The period is almost over. Maybe he should come back after school when there's more time. But he goes in anyway. The man is clearly exhausted, but he still exudes good cheer. Niall opens

Colton's paper to the interview section and lays it on the desk in front of Johnson. "Have a look."

Johnson reads, then, after a few seconds he looks up. "What is this?"

"Colton Chadwick's outline for his research paper. He's writing about white supremacy and he's interviewed all these people he claims to know."

Johnson reads a little more. "Hm."

"I thought I should alert you. It makes me nervous because I'm not sure where his sympathies lie. After what happened on the beach, you know?"

"Hm."

"His mother said he fell in with the wrong people at his last school, but she didn't elaborate. Do you know more?"

"I can't share that, Niall. I understand your concern, but we can't be policing the opinions of our students. They're free to express what they want."

"Even hateful ideas?"

"Unfortunately, yes. The first amendment applies to high school students. As long as they're not harming anyone. If there had been specific incidents involving him it would be different, of course. And it looks as if he's quoting others, not espousing these ideas himself."

"I don't know . . . I worry that . . ."

"What? Do you know something you're not telling me?"

In a split second he evaluates what it would mean to mention the Vaseline incident and lose Trinity's trust. "No. Not really. I'm just worried. Someone wrote H8s in the dust on my car the other day. That might be relevant."

"H8?"

"A white supremacist reference to Hitler."

"Oh, right, yes. So, you think Colton might be involved with some of these organizations?"

"I don't know. I just . . ."

"I'll have a chat with him."

"If you do, please don't mention me or his paper. He's already upset with me. He has a photo of me and Ms. White on his phone and he's been taunting me with it. As if . . ."

Johnson nods. "I appreciate your vigilance. Just focus on your classes, and I'll take care of the rest. Have a good holiday."

It takes Niall a moment to remember the holiday Johnson is referring to. Right, Thanksgiving.

30

The world looked different without Francis in it. A funeral was held for him, and he was buried in the monastery's small plot. After that the brothers returned to their daily routine. Niall searched for signs of sorrow or distress on their faces, but he found none that matched his own. Was he the only one affected, or had they learned to conceal their sorrow, convert it into deeper devotion? Francis was, to him, not only a dear friend but a missed opportunity. He wished he had spent more time with Francis. He mourned all the years he hadn't even known Francis. He yearned to have known him on the outside, to have seen him perform, to have taken long walks with him at the seashore, to have cooked dinner with him and laughed. Francis had been taken from him just as their friendship was flourishing. There could have been so much more. There was no one else Niall could confide in, now that the Abbot didn't seem trustworthy.

He went to the cemetery once a day, usually in the evening, sometimes at daybreak. He cleaned the debris that had gathered on the simple stone over Francis's grave. Then he stood there, praying, sometimes reciting one of the psalms, speaking to Francis in his mind. Francis had lived only sixty-seven years, not very old these days.

"Missing your boyfriend, Brother Anselm?" Thomas sneaked

up behind him a week after Francis's death like a ghost risen from one of the graves.

Niall didn't move, didn't speak. He was aware of lacking protection now that Francis was gone. Not that Francis had ever done anything actively to protect Niall, but in addition to being a friend, he'd been paternal. Now, without Francis, Niall felt helpless as an orphaned child.

"I never understood what you saw in him. He was a buffoon. A joke of a man. Not worth wasting your time on."

Thomas had come to stand next to him, and Niall was enveloped in his vetiver scent. Niall's heat ballooned. He turned and walked to the far side of the cemetery, stopping by the stone wall and staring out over the pasture, desperate to be left alone. But Thomas was behind him again. An automaton, Niall walked away once more, this time leaving the cemetery and heading to his room. Thomas trailed in his wake.

"You should talk to me for a change. You might come to see things differently."

Niall closed the door to his chamber and, stiff, sat on the bed. Thomas remained at the door. Niall sensed his invasive presence.

The door opened a crack. "I know you came into my quarters, by the way. Stop kidding yourself." The door clicked shut.

Niall sat still until he was sure Thomas was gone.

A buffoon. He had to do something. He couldn't remain passive. He felt tipped into a new sense of himself as forceful.

Thomas had taken the van and would be gone overnight. Niall had no idea where Thomas went, but such overnight jaunts weren't unusual. Niall tucked the garden shears under his scapular. He closed the door quietly though no one else was around; all the other brothers were worshipping.

He'd seen it before, but still the room arrested him. The multitude of paintings and vases with fresh flowers. The rich jewel colors. The overall extravagance.

He lay on his back on the king bed and sank into the soft mattress and velvet bedspread, splaying his legs, closing his eyes, imagining himself in a European palace. The smell of vetiver rose from the bedding. With Thomas gone he could spend the night here if he chose to.

After a while he rose, found the white robe in the wardrobe and lay it across the bed, stretching out the sleeves so it resembled a human form, a chalk drawing on the pavement. Someone existing only in memory. The shears, made for powering through tough branches, sliced easily through the woolen fabric. He cut strips, working quickly, then tore the strips into random irregular scraps which he tossed to the center of the carpet where they made a pleasing pile. The other brothers were in the chapel, too far away to hear, but he heard them in his head, their voices pure and righteous, devout men praising God.

He took a few more things from the chest of drawers: some neatly folded silk shirts and cashmere sweaters. Where and when did Thomas wear such things? Some secret outside life?

Niall took his time with each item, cutting off the sleeves then making strips of everything so there was no chance of repair. Piles of colored fabric covered the carpet. He lay back on the bed, waiting for satisfaction to take hold. He remembered stomping on Liam's LEGOs, the shame he had felt after. Now he felt no shame.

He rose and went to the kitchen and laid out the glassware. He smashed goblets and water glasses on the marble countertop. Then he took the plates and hurled them against the slate floor. Shards of glass and ceramic littered the slate as if the place had been bombed.

He retired to the bed again, feeling better. That was enough. About to leave, he glanced at the bedside table where an ornate blue-and-red blown glass goblet held the dregs of some red wine. He hadn't come here for this, but why not—the coup de grâce.

He took the goblet to the bathroom, rinsed it, held it over the toilet and relieved himself, filling the goblet to half an inch from the lip. He wiped the outside clean and returned it to the bedside table, pausing to admire the purple tint of his urine.

He lay on the bed one last time, hoping Francis could see him, then thinking of Liam again. Liam would never have done this. But he wasn't Liam. He rose and exited as quietly as he had entered, slipping back, unseen, into the remaining days of his sacred life.

31

The beach at 6 a.m. is still dark and quietly cold. Little movement except for the gulls and the lisping waves. A spray of light from the casinos tosses shadows across the sand. A slight orange glow to the east; the sun readying to punch the sky. Niall spots the spindly legs of the pier, then the lifeguard tower. A black-clad figure leans against it, insouciant. He wears a white beanie. Niall would recognize this boy's posture anywhere.

Colton looks down the beach and up to the boardwalk then strolls to Niall until they stand only a few feet from one another.

"Hey." Colton's greeting sounds like that of a business associate, a drug dealer maybe, someone dubious about the benefits of negotiation.

"Good morning," Niall says though it still feels like night. Now what? Colton called this meeting. His email was furious. He couldn't *believe* that Niall had gone to Johnson about a dumb paper. Johnson told Colton to come see him immediately after practice. Johnson has betrayed Niall, but anger is useless now. *Be polite,* he tells himself. *You are not unjustified. Just explain yourself.*

"Two-faced," Colton says. "You try to make nice. You tell me my project is A material and then you go and report me because you think I'm a danger to the school? Because of a *fucking paper?* Jeesh."

"I understand that . . . But you have to see how it looks."

"No, I don't *see how it looks,* Monk O'Malley."

"It looks as if you might be affiliated with people who are a threat to the school."

"I was *doing research.* I was writing *the fucking paper you wanted us to write?!* You need to study the law, Monk-man."

The sun has breached the horizon, making the water a silvery-blue and silhouetting Manhattan, inviting and tranquil. It transports Niall to his upcoming journey, to hearing the Abbot's message, a faint whisper on his voicemail. *I thought you should know. You two were so close.*

"You think I'm bad, don't you? A neo-Nazi who wants to shoot up the people who don't agree with me?"

"No."

"Oh, get out of here. Of course you do. You have since the moment I walked into your classroom. Don't you believe in free speech? The First Amendment? You don't know a *damn thing* about me."

The Abbot said nothing about how long Thomas had or what he was dying from. Maybe he knew such ambiguity would function as a summons.

Colton turns so his back faces Niall, and he yanks off his white beanie. He lifts the shank of blond hair that hangs behind his head and lowers the neckline of his shirt to expose the back of his shoulder. The sun becomes a flashlight spotlighting the space between spine and shoulder where there's a tattoo, a shakily drawn Celtic cross.

Colton speaks in a low monotone, staring out across the water, squinting into the sunrise, glancing occasionally behind him to the boardwalk.

The story he tells sounds apocryphal.

He was at a prep school, the most recent of the several fancy ones from which he was booted. He'd found a group of boys he thought were like himself: independent thinkers, people who preferred not to blindly follow rules that didn't make sense. They were all from rich families, of course, because that was who attended that school.

There was a party in the basement of Jimbo's family's country house. It was after midnight—the parents had gone to sleep hours before—and the boys were all drunk and rowdy, ready for hijinks. They laughed about giving each other tattoos. He didn't know those boys well—he'd only been at the school for a couple of months—but they weren't bad boys, just boys who liked alcohol and high risk. There was one boy, Deeder, who Colton avoided. Deeder hung on the edges of their activities, sitting in corners, making sarcastic, sometimes downright mean wisecracks. Colton had spent two hours at Deeder's house once, and Deeder had spent the whole time showing Colton Civil War simulations he enacted with small figurines. He talked about all the battles in detail, and Colton quickly grew bored and got out of there. After that they kept their distance from each other. Colton was pretty sure Deeder, who wasn't very fit, was jealous of him. As for the Civil War simulations, he didn't think much about that until later.

Colton was especially drunk that night. He passed out on the couch. When he returned to consciousness he was on his belly on the floor, his shoulder screaming with pain. Deeder was tattooing him. When Colton realized what was happening he resisted, tried get up, but the other boys held him down while Deeder finished his work.

When they released him, Colton stumbled to the bathroom, his shoulder awash with pain. He vomited then tried to use the mirror to examine the damage. The mirror wouldn't show him anything.

In one of the most humiliating moments of his life, he called his parents at four in the morning asking them to pick him up. His father came, glanced at his suppurating shoulder, and drove him home in silence. His mother, a demon of indignation, flying around in her robe, dressed his wound, railing at the other boys, railing at Colton. *What were you thinking? Who are these friends of yours?* She said she would report them to the headmaster, but Colton begged her not to. If she did they would torture him—he would be dead meat. She wanted to take him to the emergency room, but Colton refused to go.

He never went back to that school and hasn't seen Deeder since. Only one of the other boys reached out to say he was sorry. They were too drunk to know what Deeder was doing, the boy said. Deeder answered Colton's rabid email, saying: *Joke, buddy. It was just a joke.*

Colton says the tattoo changed his life. Despite his efforts to conceal it, certain people spot it anyway, and jump to conclusions, approach him like a member of a tribe. He had to extricate himself from a few sticky situations. And by the way, he says, he's going to have it removed at winter break.

He stops talking, pulls his shirt over the tattoo, and restores the beanie to his head. They both look out at the distant skyscrapers of Manhattan which might, from this distance, be a fake city, full of promises that will never be met. The sun sears their eyeballs. A breeze comes up. A jogger passes them at an impressive clip. Niall pictures himself joining the jogger and escaping down the beach.

Colton turns to Niall.

"You don't know squat about me. If you don't want to believe me, that's your problem, but don't go accusing people without the facts." He swivels with the precision of a dancer, struts up the beach toward the boardwalk, and disappears down an alleyway next to the movie theater.

Niall doesn't return to his car right away. He needs to walk. He heads south down the beach, energized by the relentlessly brightening sun and the rising wind, and by the increasingly restless water which seems ready to become serious surf, rock-and-rolling into the new day.

Part Two

32

Weaving through the rabid holiday traffic, he speeds, swears, swerves, trying to offload the rage Colton has transferred onto him. How can a high school boy terrify him so much? But of course boys Colton's age are more likely than most to commit acts of violence. He's right to be afraid. *Check your facts, Monk-man.* He tries to replace these thoughts of Colton with fuzzy images of a dying Thomas which shiver on the road ahead of him like a mirage. He shouldn't be driving.

He cracks a hardboiled egg on the steering wheel, peels it one-handed so a confetti of tiny shells scatters over the seat and gearshift. He takes a bite and shell-shards settle in his molars. He tosses the rest of the egg out the window, inciting a glare from a passing car. The phone in his crotch vibrates. Trinity. *Gotta talk.*

The northbound Garden State Highway is clogged with too many cars. An enraged driver behind the wheel of a behemoth Ford truck roars past at tornado speed, clipping Niall's front bumper, jolting his spinal cord, dislodging his eyeballs. As he tries to regain control of his body and car, the truck is sucked into traffic, untraceable, only Niall's rattled nerves testament to its passing.

The day is like every other Thanksgiving holiday he remembers, chilly and damp and overcast, the backdrop for a weekend of overeating and bickering. *I'm not feeling well,* he told his mother, and that was true, wasn't it? She took it calmly. *All this food,* she said. *But I can freeze it.* His mother is too good, too understanding, too willing to overlook his foibles.

At a rest area he examines his bumper, rubbing his fingers over the dinged fender, a nick much smaller than the jolt to his heart. What is it with people these days? It isn't only Colton who scares him—everyone is on a vengeful tear. He uses the restroom, eyeing the other men warily, the sound of his urination bringing on exhaustion like a sudden drenching rain. Back in his car he thinks of turning around, spending the holiday weekend catching up on grading, having coffee with Trinity, sleeping as much as he can. He owes Thomas nothing, does he?

He replays the Abbot's voicemail. He almost deleted it, an unrecognizable number and a voice almost too soft to hear. *You two were so close. I thought you should know.* Did the Abbot really think he and Thomas were close?

He gasses up and continues on, drawn by an imperative he doesn't understand, hours later approaching the Massachusetts/Vermont border where he exits and looks for a place to stay. Two motels turn him away—no vacancy. Why aren't people with their families and friends for the holiday? The traffic thins and dusk quickly darkens the woods and pastures. He begins to imagine sleeping in his car. Then, appearing out of the night like a manse on a dark moor, is the two-story Cozy Corner Motel. They give him their last room, a room for the handicapped on the ground floor. It's not a location that suggests vacation, but it's a place to sleep.

He pulls the flimsy curtains against the orange lights of the parking lot and collapses onto the bed—a brief nap before he goes on the quest for food. Someone clomps around in the room above him. A toilet flushes. More clomping. He sleeps.

33

He jerks awake. It's 10:45 p.m. He's famished, wired. He leaps to the floor, digs for his remaining boiled egg and devours it. He should have thought to stop for food—nothing will be open now.

He checks his phone—nothing of consequence. Reception is weak. He takes a moment to answer Trinity's text—*On a road trip. Back in touch soon*—then steps outside.

The motel's neon sign has been turned off. The darkness thrills him. The sky has cleared and is crazy with stars. It's so quiet it's hard to believe the motel is filled with people. His body thrums with energy as if he's had a full night of sleep. He sniffs. Something here nourishes him. The smell of decomposing November leaves. The humidity. The rich dirt. Even the mountains seem to effuse a smell. It's so different from the petroleum-riddled air of New Jersey.

He flies through the night, windows down, wind rushing through his hair, down the back of his neck as if someone is stroking him. A half-moon sculpts the bare tree branches so each tree looks like a person with distinct mien and attitude, some scowling, some smiling, some massive, some stunted. It is said they all converse through their roots, assisting each other in staying alive. Lucky trees. A pleasant delirium fills him. He might be passing through Alaska, Romania, New Zealand. The world is his.

An intersection pops into view with a brightly-lit gas station and a convenience store, an oasis of fuel and sugar, but both are closed. He breezes onto a larger road, not one he recognizes. Light whispers up from the porches of a few farm houses set back from the road. The marks on Colton's shoulder reappear to him, as if they've been etched on his own retinas. He chants quietly, *Kyrie Eleison,* trying to unsee things, pushing Colton into the past, all that anger and hate and fear he has no use for. Gone.

The night swaddles him, and he seems to be in the cockpit of a plane, not a car, swooping over everything, even his own life. He remembers belonging here in the bosom of these gentle mountains and pastures. He shouldn't have left. He half-forgets why he did.

The familiar sign and stone pillars are lit. It was not his intention to come here at night. How far has he driven? Maybe twenty or thirty miles from his motel.

He stops on the opposite side of the road and regards the sign, the stone pillars, the long driveway, a few lights in the distance. His heartbeat is syncopated. He should wait and return in daylight because what he is about to do is bad for his heart, bad for his health, bad for his soul. It might be illegal. Of course it's illegal.

Nevertheless, he steps from his car, crosses the road, passes between the pillars, follows the paved quarter-mile driveway, hearing his footsteps resounding clear to the mountains. He'll only be a minute, a quick look-see, then back to his car, his motel, his mini-vacation. Maybe he'll pay a legitimate visit in daylight.

A trio of cows, awakened on the other side of the fence, approaches to investigate. *It's okay, it's just me—remember me?— nothing to worry about.* They watch him without retreating.

The pavement gives way to the gravel parking lot, and the paths leading to the clusters of buildings. A motion light clicks on, sighting him and limning the structures: chapel, refectory, dormitory, guest cottages, barns, administration building. Many as old as the early 1800s, some built during the WPA, buildings put together with industry and devotion now reflected in their enduring stonework. He walks on the grass to avoid the light, hugging the perimeter of the lot. Halting in the shadows, he listens. Nothing but a slight seepage beneath his feet. Everyone but the most insomniac is asleep now. The motion light goes off, and he begins to move again, skirting the administration building where Abbot Jerome has his quarters. In the building behind that the other brothers sleep. Men capable of committing their lives to God and making peace with the challenges of solitude and silence. He remembers, when he first arrived, noting the smooth skin of most of the brothers, regardless of their age. Even Francis, pock-marked, carried a benign look. It was as if they'd all been touched with divine makeup. He remembers checking his own skin a few months into his residence to see if it had improved (it hadn't). Brother Thomas was the only notable exception, his face sanguine, his cheeks and forehead and neck and the skin beneath his eyes visibly ravaged by whatever excesses he'd indulged in before arriving at the monastery.

It suddenly occurs to him he has no idea if Thomas is here. If he's close to death, as the Abbot has said, he might be in a hospital—or a hospice. He stares at the thick stone walls of the residential hall. Beyond the dim light at the entrance there isn't any illumination. He continues on. Quiet. Stealthy. The grass is wet and muddy. He stumbles over a pile of rocks, catches himself against the wall.

Navigating like a sightless climber, he proceeds, hand over hand. He rounds the corner of the building, stops. A few feet away is one of the windows of Thomas's extravagant dwelling. He moves toward it, gloveless hands numbed by the cold stone. He arrives beneath the window. He's too low to see in. He backtracks, palpating the ground for rocks, gathering them into a pile beneath the window. Gingerly, he stands on the pile which elevates him to the perfect height. He grips the window ledge and presses his face against the glass, blinks, blinks, blinks. Dim shapes begin to clarify themselves. It's the same elegantly-appointed room. And there in the bed, propped up with multiple pillows, is the same dark-bearded man.

A light snaps on.

He jerks back, topples from his perch, falls hard on the ground, twisting, landing on his leg. A sharp pain. A well of darkness.

34

He opens his eyes, closes them. On top of profound silence bells chime faintly then fade into silence again. Sweat pools in his eyes, and a chill girdles his torso. Wave after wave of an intense feeling he can't name swallows the lower half of his body. He opens his eyes again. Blades of grass graze his cheek. He stares at the solid gray stone of the building, everything else subsumed in darkness, hearing the bells again.

He remembers falling. He remembers a light going on. He remembers seeing Thomas's black beard. He might have been hallucinating. He has no idea what time it is, how much time has elapsed since he peered through the window. The encompassing feeling, which he now understands as pain, comes and goes, a faraway pulsing, almost not belonging to him. He heaves himself to sitting, inviting a more serious surge of pain. He waits for it to ebb. He tastes blood on his lip. He tries to remember where he's left his car.

Scooting his bottom closer to the wall, he leans the weight of his upper body into it and wills himself to standing, hovering upright for only a second before he collapses. Face down. Pain as a hammer-shaped flame pounds his legs, as if they have merged into a tail. He's a grotesque merman. Not lovely like Lluvia. How he wishes she were here, though the thought of her fills him with shame.

He plants his elbows into the grass and raises his belly to hump himself forward, tail dragging, inch by inch, cursing the pain then laying his forehead down in the wet grass like a supplicant, allowing the pain to wash over him. He shivers, toe to scalp. His car is out there somewhere. The night is endless.

It's too dark to see if he's making any progress. His torso rattles with cold; his teeth knock against each other so hard he fears he might break them. He could be killing himself in this endeavor. Then Thomas can gloat. He should have stayed in the motel room to sleep and rise refreshed to enjoy his mini-vacation. Away from the job that addles him; away from the students who scare him; away from Colton's pernicious shape-shifting presence.

Soldiers in the trenches have endured far worse—and Jesus, of course, carrying his own cross, stoned, nailed, what pain that must have been—but those people didn't bring their pain upon themselves.

Hump. Hump. Hump.

The skin of his belly must be shredding. Beneath it his organs vibrate as if they're preparing to pop and spill. Pain sears his thigh. A sound fills him, summons him. The bells again, solemn and sure, deep at first then laced with harmonics that resonate higher and higher. Such a familiar sound, whispering through darkness. His life has always been ruled by one kind of bell or another. *To remind us that all things pass away*, Merton said of bells. Vigils or lauds, who knows, he only knows it's time to pray. He has no breath for speaking aloud, but he intones some remembered words in his head: *If you faint in the day of adversity your strength is small."* Proverbs 24:10. Energy leaks then gushes. He's gone again.

His mother stands over him, shaking him awake. *Niall. Anselm. Niall. Anselm. Niall.* His mother has never called him Anselm.

Morning light pierces his lids, too bright, too cheerful, the birds too loud. *Mother, please, let me sleep.* She kneels next to him, a blanket woven of warmth and worry. *Can you hear me?* He wants to tell her it hurts, but his voice is absent.

No, not his mother, someone else with the dulcet presence of his mother. *We can't let you . . .* Someone holds his hand and the sentience of his entire body rushes to that hand. He wants to thank the owner of the hand. He wants the hand to keep holding him. He wants to say: *Don't go!*

The ambulance workers turn him from belly to back and ease him onto a stretcher. Brother Joseph stands over him, an ancient man with the voice of an angel. Behind him, light tints the sky pink and purple. Abbot Jerome cocks his head to one side, face puckered with concern. A blur of spectators, other brothers, swaying like water.

"Bless you," says the Abbot. Joseph pats his shoulder.

He is spirited off in the ambulance, drifting in and out of sleep.

35

He jerks awake at the summoning of the bells. Propping himself up, he looks out at the winking dawn, the familiar sight of the brothers flocking to prayer along the paths, their robes fluttering on a light breeze. He's here again. Unfathomable.

He lies back down, enervated by the brief hospital stay, brain fuzzy with drugs, pain in his right leg, remote but present as far off lightning. The recent events return to him, falling slowly into place. His meeting with Colton, the drive north, the motel, the fall, his two—or was it three?—days in the hospital to operate on his broken leg and make sure the wound on his thigh didn't get infected. He arrived here last night under cover of darkness as if in bringing him here the Abbot was doing something covert. It's kind of the Abbot to let him recuperate here, but he hoped to be here with more agency, to rectify things, to be an adult.

He's in one of the monastery's three guest cottages, used most often by civilians coming for short retreats. He never had the occasion to enter one of these cottages before. It's a standalone stonework building: a large open space including a sleeping area with a king bed, sitting area, bathroom, and kitchenette, windows in front and back. It's far more comfortable and better situated than his motel room was, and the Abbot said someone will bring him meals, as well as take care of changing his dressing, but . . .

He detected the trace of a wince, a sneer, but still he agreed to go up the drumlin with Thomas that sultry June day because this wince and sneer were half-obscured by a veneer of gentleness. A walk. Only a walk. Maybe an offer of truce.

So he agreed and followed Thomas down the driveway and across the road to an unfamiliar path through the pine woods, the sky a cloudless blue but hazed with humidity that made his robe stick to the back of his thighs as he tromped uphill, the pine-needle path soft and fragrant, the cicadas chanting like a chorus of tiny monks in the growing heat of the day. Silence between them. It had been two weeks since the last urine incident—Niall's retort—and since then they'd avoided each other. He'd been wrestling too long alone with the darkness enveloping his soul. It was time to make peace, become the good man he'd always sought to become.

Half an hour they walked. The midday heat thrummed around them as if they were inside the lungs of a mastodon, something throbbing to extinction, the hazy sun a taunt between the pine boughs, their necks sweating.

The trees opened onto a promontory with a view of the ripening valley, dressed in pale spring green, alive with the promise of fecundity. He stood uncertainly beside Thomas, both of them gazing out, feigning obliviousness to one another though the past shawled them and whispered up from their feet. Niall began to relax, hopeful they might untangle themselves, purify the air between them, move into a life where neither would torture the other, and they would both carry on as better men, the evil within them dispelled.

A squirrel on a nearby branch fell to the ground and scurried between them. Thomas turned, his feet, staunch fence posts, situating themselves in the needled dirt. They were only a few feet from one another. Thomas worried his robe and scapular as if he wished to remove them. His voice was low, a sound that seemed to arrive from deep in the woods, like the protest of a waking bear.

"You have a choice. A kiss—or I wallop you. Which?"

A stare-down ensued, all of Thomas's power enshrined in his beard and unblinking blue eyes, beautiful and terrible. His expression was fixed in unreadable repose, his question hovering on the humidity. Impossible to answer. Intended to trap. Niall was a wisp of a man, David to Thomas's Goliath, startled and unprepared.

Branches cracked under the weight of yet another squirrel who, miscalculating his weight, had thudded to the ground.

The stare-down continued. The heat throbbed on. Thomas's eyelids lowered so for a moment he looked relaxed as a sunning lizard until a harsh whisper sprang from him. "Don't pretend you don't want me." He lunged forward, lips in the lead. He seized Niall's shoulders, held him still.

Niall wrested himself from under Thomas's grip and, as if an alarm had sounded, the punches began, both of them clenching fists, swinging arms, fully engaged. The outpouring of years of suppressed anger, envy, lust and longing. Niall, smaller and slimmer and not nearly as strong, was destined to lose to the feral force of Thomas, but anger empowered him, and he leveled some spot-on punches. Still, in the end he went down, fetal and moaning in dirt and pine needles. He didn't want Thomas. He'd never wanted Thomas.

Thomas stood, straightened, brushed himself off, and headed down the path, leaving Niall alone. The following week his mother came for him.

It shames him now to remember how easily he was seduced into violence that day. He'd never been in a physical fight before, had shrunk from them all his life. He hardly knew how to punch, but at that moment instinct had prevailed. His bruised face labeled him as a man who had fallen far from God, incapable of turning the other cheek. In the days after, he saw Thomas only from a distance, and it appeared that his face had not been harmed at all. How humiliating it was for Niall to sit in the chapel and the refectory, his own bruised face announcing his rift with God. He made himself attend every communal activity as punishment. But he kept his gaze averted from the other brothers, feeling their judgment raining down on him though no one but the Abbot said a word about what had happened, and even he said very little. A public chastising was the Cistercian tradition, but that would involve reprimanding Thomas too, and by then Niall understood the complications of that—Thomas had never been subject to the usual rules. Niall tried to accept his own disrepute gracefully, but it was brutal, and he developed chest pains, a hurt in his heart. In the silence of his room he went over and over what had happened. Thomas was wrong. Niall had never desired Thomas—he'd never desired any man. It bothered him that Thomas didn't believe him.

He should have gone to Thomas to work things out, say he was sorry, but that would have been lying. All the strange history between them, years of it, had hardened him. The rage that Thomas always uncovered in him hadn't cooled, would never cool, he feared. He couldn't bring himself to apologize.

A knock on the door and a young man in civilian clothes enters with a breakfast tray. He lays the tray on Niall's lap and introduces himself. He's a postulant named Noah, twenty-seven; he's been here for four months after several years on a commune in Vermont. He will be tending to Niall, he says. He has been trained as a nurse and can change the dressing on Niall's thigh wound. He will also be bringing meals and whatever else Niall needs.

Niall nods. "Thank you." He hopes Noah will leave, but the young man lingers, hovering timidly near the bed, unsure whether to stay or go.

"Okay," Noah finally says. "I'll come back later to change your dressing. If you need anything, text me. The Abbot gave me permission for that—texting with you."

The breakfast is impressive: a cheese-and-mushroom omelet, two sausages, buttered toast made from the crusty whole-grain homemade monastery bread, slices of orange festooned with pomegranate seeds, and black tea. It is much more elegant than the simple fare the monks eat. Do visitors always get treated so well? Having eaten almost nothing in the hospital, he devours everything on his plate and gives himself over to asleep again.

He dozes all day, his slumber only interrupted by Noah's comings and goings with lunch, medications, a new dressing, the bells, the damn bells swirling into a helix with his pain, marking off the passage of time, acting like ambassadors of his conscience. Each time he wakes he remembers his broken leg, and it feels like the demarcation of a new day, so by evening when Noah brings him dinner, and he's finally alert, it feels as if a week might have passed.

He forces himself out of bed and with Noah's help uses his crutches to get to the sitting area where his dinner tray is on the coffee table. He situates himself on the couch facing Noah who perches on the edge of the easy chair as if he's an invited guest. Another impressive meal: baked salmon, mashed potatoes, kale sautéed with onions, a green salad, buttered bread, tea, and custard.

"Go ahead, eat," Noah says.

Niall absorbs the fullness of Noah for the first time. He appears to be so much more youthful than Niall though only a few years separate them. Has he also been bait for Thomas? Bushy brown hair and smooth olive skin; a lean, muscular body; the look of a woodsman, accustomed to solitude, easily surprised and eager to please. *My personal assistant,* Niall thinks with amusement.

He takes a bite of the salmon which is moist and well-seasoned, but he has a hard time eating with Noah watching him, and he lays down his fork.

"How are you liking it here?"

"Good. It's good. Sometimes the quiet drives me crazy, but I'm getting used to it."

"What brought you here?"

"Well, you know, the usual. Wanting to devote my life to God. Isn't that what brings most people?"

"Maybe."

"You were here I know. What brought you?"

"I'm still working that out."

Noah nods as if Niall has said something profound when it was only an evasion. "Why are you here now?" Noah asks.

Niall evaluates Noah. How unfettered and open he seems to be, asking the unanswerable. Niall shakes his head and turns to his food.

"Unfinished business, I guess you could say." Again Noah nods, absorbing Niall's words. "How does it feel to be the youngest one here?"

Noah hesitates, frowns. "It's—different. On the commune, everyone was around my age. To be so much younger—well, it makes you think about different things. You know?"

"What do you mean?"

"Well, like death, I guess. With so many old men around, you know?"

"Have you gotten to know any of the brothers well?"

"Not really."

"Not Brother Thomas?"

"I feel so bad for him."

"Because he's dying?"

"Well, yeah. We all die, but to die *that way—ALS*. God, it's my personal nightmare. Getting weaker and weaker. Finally not being able to walk or talk or eat. Your brain locked in. No cure. No real treatments. That's what Thomas told me. I mean, really, isn't that the worst way to go?"

ALS. Why hadn't the Abbot mentioned this in his voicemail? Niall tries to conceal his surprise. "I wouldn't know."

"Yeah, well . . ." Noah shrugs. "Terrible luck, I think."

Noah's departure plunges Niall into a deeper silence. He stares at the beautiful meal, unable to eat, thinking about Thomas.

36

Having slept all day, Niall doesn't sleep that night, thinking of Thomas dying of ALS, becoming an inert piece of flesh housing a still-active consciousness. If disease is a metaphor or an expression of psychic pain or an indication of a soul out of alignment, what is the psychic or soul disruption for ALS? The weakening muscles can only be, in Thomas's case, a direct result of his hubris. But does it alter Niall's intent in coming here? Is dying of ALS any different from dying of cancer? His mission is still the same, isn't it?

He sits up in bed, his broken tibia and the wound on his thigh throbbing past the pain meds. The darkness outside devours him, weakening him, making all his bones feel brittle, his neurons fuzzy. He tenses each muscle, one by one, forehead to toe, testing his vigor. In his mind's eye, he has sprouted a dense dark beard like Thomas's beard; his eyes are cold and unblinking like Thomas's eyes. His own mean streak is the only thing surviving as his body languishes. A terrible thought seizes him: He and Thomas have become twins, linked as twins are, and he, too, is succumbing to ALS. He can't sleep now—sleep will annihilate him—so he remains sitting, eyes open, spectral versions of his diseased self-parading before him.

Daybreak could not be more of a relief. He fixes his eyes on the horizon, drinking in the light, feeling like himself again. He tests his muscles, tensing and releasing them, and they seem to be fine. Exhausted, he sleeps.

The knocking penetrates his dreams. It's Noah with his break-fast tray, accompanied by the Abbot who has come for a visit. It's early for socializing, but Niall, trying to rally, looks around for his crutches.

"No, no," says the Abbot. "Stay where you are."

Noah lays the tray on his lap and disappears, leaving Niall alone with the Abbot. Niall, barely awake, stares down at the food. French toast, applesauce, bacon, orange slices, and tea. The sight of it overwhelms him; the Abbot's benign gaze overwhelms him; the weight of his pulsing leg in its cast overwhelms him. This inability to make sense of anything—is this how Thomas feels?

"Do you mind if I sit?"

Niall shakes his head, fine, and the Abbot takes a seat at the end of the bed, making himself comfortable. "Are you feeling better? Is Noah treating you well?"

Niall nods.

"Go ahead. Eat."

Niall sips the tea.

"So, you've come back?"

Yes, he's here, back in some way.

"I know you came to see Thomas. But I have to ask—why did you come at night, risking injury as you did?"

Niall stares at the Abbot, incredulous. Is it possible the Abbot knows nothing of what transpired between him and Thomas? How can that be after Niall asked for the Abbot's assistance so many times? And everyone saw the repercussions of their fight. Why would the Abbot play dumb?

"No, don't bother to explain. I know you two had a complicated relationship. But I'm glad you're here. I know he cares about you a lot. He wanted you to come though he couldn't bring himself to say so directly . . . Eat. Eat."

Niall looks at the food warily, and the Abbot chuckles. "Okay, I'll back off. The Jewish mother role isn't a good fit for me . . . What I'd really like to know is—are you here for other reasons as well? Is it possible you'd like to come back for good? Maybe you've found the outside world to be a harrowing place?"

From the depths of his grogginess, Niall finds his voice. "No." An abject lie in answer to a leading question—of course the world *is* a harrowing place.

"Then you're fulfilled in your new life?"

"I teach young people—teenagers. And they teach me, of course. I'm hoping I can, I don't know, affect them a little. Make them into good people, you know?"

"A challenging task, but noble. You teach history?"

"Yes."

"A knowledge of history can change us if we're open to its lessons."

"Some of them are open."

"If you reach one person it's worthwhile."

The Abbot scratches his beard, an affectation Niall remembers well.

"The only reason I'm asking you this is because I spoke to your principal, and he alluded to difficulties with some of your students."

"You spoke to Dr. Johnson? How did you . . . ?"

"I had to let him know you wouldn't be fit for teaching for a while."

Niall's brain is seriously disordered. The Abbot has spoken with Johnson. How did he know where to find Johnson? How much has Johnson said? His worlds are colliding, tectonic plates squeezing him in the fissure between.

The Abbot laughs. "Don't look so panicked. Your mother—I talked to your mother. Relax, Niall. Your principal has arranged for a substitute. It's all fine."

All fine. No worries. How he has hated such reassurances when they're always false.

"I'm glad you're satisfied in your new life. But if you ever change your mind and want to return, you're welcome. You know that, I hope. No burned bridges. We loved you once, and we will go on loving you. And we need young people like you and Noah. To help us survive." He crosses himself as Niall absorbs the *aha* moment. The Order won't survive without young blood.

"God bless you and speedy healing." The Abbot winks and filches an orange slice from Niall's plate. "Oh, check in on Thomas when you feel ready to move around. He's expecting you. But be careful—snow is in the forecast."

37

In the silence following the Abbot's departure, Niall remains still, smelling the bacon and the French toast but unable to eat. The Abbot has talked to his mother and to Johnson! He is lobbying for Niall's return to the monastery. What a busybody he is. He has no business trying to manage Niall this way.

Exhausted as he is, there is no way Niall can sleep. He needs to get up, get out, execute the business he came here to, be done with it, then get his mother to come for him. Energized, he shoots off a text to Noah, takes a few bites of bacon, shoves the tray aside, and flings off the covers.

Niall and Noah stand on the pathway just outside the cottage, Noah's hand behind Niall's back. The air is cold, the sky a gray grimace promising snow, the ground suffused with the fervid hush of monks at work. This is Niall's first foray out on his crutches. He shifts his weight, straightens his spine, and sniffs the chill cleansing air, nourishing his resolve. He will clear the air at last.

"You sure you're up for this?" Noah asks.

Niall nods and lurches forward, Noah scuttling beside him. When Niall comes to the main path, he hesitates. A right turn would take him to the monks' dormitory where Thomas has his elegant quarters. Niall has told Noah he intends to visit Thomas, but now he heads left up the slight incline that leads to the barn, the chapel, the cemetery. Noah follows in steadfast support, no questions asked.

Niall will stretch his legs then turn around and head to see Thomas. The muted sounds of activity swaddle them, composing the silence not interrupting it: the tink of metal on metal, a lowing cow, the van taking off. Niall and Noah have arrived in front of the chapel, empty at this time of the morning.

"You want to go in?" Noah asks.

Niall declines with a shake of his head. He has no relationship with God, and entering the chapel would make that painfully obvious. He gazes up to the cemetery where Francis lies buried. A small bird he can't identify swoops over the hill's crest and a numinous force traveling in the bird's wake touches his heart like a plucked string. Fortifying, almost a voice.

38

Leaning on his crutches, he hesitates just inside the chapel entrance looking around, incredulous. It can't possibly be the same place where he spent so many hours chanting and praying for five years. He's always loved the tranquility of this chapel, remodeled sometime in the last century with a modernist aesthetic in mind, but he has never been so taken aback by its beauty. Wintery morning light whirls through the stained-glass windows, trembling and flashing about the space like something alive, illuminating first this then that with muted colors, in some places depositing small bright pools like half-hidden Easter eggs. What splendor! The honey wood of the pews and the pulpit, the immense blocks of quarried stone that form the walls, pale gray and textured as a topographical map; the polished light wood floor; the stained-glass windows that line the sides of the chapel depicting the stations of the cross; directly in front of the chapel, behind the pulpit, two clear-glass windows with abstract designs, for the worshipper to find in it whatever message he chooses; all of it sanctified by the faint perfume of melted wax and incense—how has he failed to fully appreciate these things?

He's never had the place to himself like this. It's good to be away from the claustrophobia of his cottage. He advances slowly down the center aisle, not wanting to interrupt the sacred silence with any sound of his own. He takes a seat at the end of one of the rear pews, crosses himself. He has forgotten about Noah who is still there and now leans down to whisper, "I have some things to attend to—I'll be back in half an hour. Is that okay?" Niall nods and Noah is gone so soundlessly he seems to have been wanded away.

Niall knows he has no right to be seeking help or solace from God, but here he is praying. He misses the presence of the other brothers who he could always count on to bless the space with their sonorous, authoritative voices, their command of the scripture, their knowledge of what came next. Without them, something is absent. Without them, he has no idea how to process what has happened, how to talk to God. Can God possibly assist him now in facing Thomas again, setting things right?

Thy kingdom come, thy will be done, on Earth as it is in Heaven. He has eradicated prayer from his life, and beginning again feels insincere, as if he were praying as a tourist does, the occasional church visitor, murmuring rote words, gliding over the surface of something deep. He isn't thinking of the meaning of the words, but their familiar whispered sounds soothe him a little anyway, as if he's a child surrendering to sleep as his mother reads *Goodnight Moon* for the thousandth time. The adrenaline drains away, leaving him drowsy. He stretches out on the hard wooden pew and lets himself doze. Each time his eyes open, they land on the window depicting Jesus in Gethsemane, hands pressed in prayer, forearms resting on a boulder, gaze uplifted. Behind him the stained-glass sky is a dazzling blue that wavers from brilliant cerulean to a more somber indigo as clouds scoot past outside. A dream image comes to him: himself as one of the disciples, slumbering as Jesus prays nearby; he is one of the ones too faithless to resist sleep.

A thud awakens him, the sound of his own body landing on the chapel floor in the narrow space between the rows. Feeling foolish, he checks his body for damage and tries to locate his crutches, remembers he left them resting at the end of the pew. He lifts his head, sees a man in a wheelchair in the center aisle a few feet away staring down at him.

Thomas. A year and a half can do this much to a man? He's recognizable—the beard and trenchant unblinking blue eyes—but extreme weight loss has changed the shape of his face and torso. His bones, their skin undressed, announce themselves beneath his casual civilian clothes. Cheek bones. Collar bones. The bones of his jaw and knuckles. His large head hangs forward from his stringy neck like a wrecking ball. His formerly sanguine face has paled, and his full lips remain parted. His appearance, if not attractive, is arresting for the way it's been pared down.

"Can I give you a hand?" Thomas asks.

Niall struggles to rise. He spots his crutches next to Thomas's wheelchair and Thomas, following his gaze, lifts the crutches and slowly, laboriously, extends them to Niall. Losing strength, he drops them suddenly, and they tumble onto Niall's belly. "So sorry. It's the disease. It's hard to grasp certain objects."

Niall elevates himself slowly, one hand on the bench, the other on the Bible rack which fractures and falls to the floor along with its three Bibles. He grabs the back of the pew and hoists himself to standing then maneuvers the crutches under his armpits, seething beneath Thomas's unrelenting gaze. Finally organized, he regards Thomas directly and shakes his head. "I'm a mess." Thomas nods, says nothing, rolls his wheelchair toward the door. Niall stumps along behind.

Outside, the November sun—or is it December already, yes it must be—stuns his eyes so he can't keep them open. He pauses, reels, nearly falls.

"You okay?" Thomas asks.

"Fine." Niall steps into a pocket of shade. "You surprised me."

"Surely you expected to see me at some point? Isn't that why you came here?"

Niall doesn't answer. Of course he came for this, but how has Thomas seized control? How typical of Thomas to ambush him.

"Would you like to talk?" Thomas asks. The voice is lower and less inflected than Thomas's old voice.

"Talk?"

Thomas laughs. "I know it's not what we're accustomed to doing."

Why doesn't Thomas ever blink? If he blinked he might not appear so menacing. Even in a wheelchair something about him scares Niall. He didn't want to feel this way, weak and confused and ill-prepared instead of clear and strong. The bells have begun to ring for midday prayers, almost overhead, gonging, impossibly loud as if to rearrange thought. Dizzied by the metallic sunlight reflecting off the snow, the bells, the residue of his violent dreams, he closes his eyes. The brothers will converge here soon—he can't stay for that.

He strides away from Thomas as quickly as his crutches allow.

39

Back at his cottage, Niall crawls back into bed, nauseated, cold, hot. Maybe he's coming down with something. The bells are still blaring: summoning, reproving, pointing the finger at him. He remembers his mother reciting the Poe poem about bells. *Bells, bells, bells, bells, bells, bells, bells.* There is no tintinnabulation here. No merriment. No impelling rapture. Only shrieking, jangling turbulence. He draws the covers over his head, unable to straighten his thoughts—what shame he feels that he was, yet again, so destabilized by Thomas. Maybe he's having a nervous breakdown, a psychotic episode. Except for the occasional depression, mostly in college, his mental health has been fine, but now his vision is serving up the disturbing image of a chimerical figure, half-Colton, half-Thomas, his tormentors joining together into a gargoyle-like personification of evil. *Grow up, Niall. Pull it together. Thomas no longer has power over you—he is weak and dying.*

Noah knocks and enters. "Are you okay? I couldn't find you."

"I'm fine," Niall assures him, trying to feel as fine as he says he is.

"Shall I help you go visit Thomas?"

"Not yet, thank you. I need to rest."

"Okay. Just let me know when."

He lies in bed rigid, trying to galvanize himself and let the chapel encounter go. What is the quote from Merton that meant so much to him in the past? Why can't he remember when he invoked it so often in deciding to become a teacher? His phone vibrates. Trinity.

"Hey, I can't talk long, but I have to tell you something."

"What? Are you at school?"

"Where else would I be? That photo Colton took of us? It's everywhere."

"What do you mean everywhere?"

"All over the internet. All the platforms."

"You mean Colton posted it?"

"Who else? It was on his phone. All day people have been making jokes about us being a couple."

"Oh god. But you've said we're not, right?"

"Of course. But it doesn't matter. No one believes me. Once something like that gets going, it's impossible to refute."

"It's his revenge. Colton's revenge against me about his paper."

"Look, Niall, don't freak out. We just need to ride it through. I mean, at least you've broken up with Lluvia. Look, I have to teach. We'll talk later."

Why does she always do this, hang up when he still has questions? It has begun to snow, the flakes a whorl filling his windows and, as if coordinated, the midday bells have begun to ring. Several brothers hurry up the path, their robes and the flakes swoon in a rhapsody of white.

Of course Colton intended to post that photo all along, especially after Niall told him not to, and now the perfect retaliation against Niall for reporting him to Johnson. What a despicable boy he is.

Niall pictures Lluvia seeing the photo. She is not on social media, but Flora could show it to her. What would she think of Niall and Trinity sitting on the hood of his car in the parking lot? Would she assume greater intimacy? He tries to remember the photo's details, remembers only two things: Trinity's head thrown back in hilarity and the proximity of their bodies. It meant nothing but friendship, but it looked like more. But why should it matter now that he and Lluvia are not together?

Another cluster of white-robed brothers hurries by, indistinguishable one from the other, the bells still pealing, the snow still falling and picking up speed. Who is orchestrating this alabaster concert?

In a few minutes the bells will cease and the brothers will stand shoulder-to-shoulder in the warmth of the chapel, changing in unison, coordinating their voices like the young basketball players in Cambridge coordinated their bodies in pursuit of a single goal. He shivers, stricken by a sudden longing for Lluvia. Her cheerfulness, her compact body, her certain sense of self. He never deserved her. He hopes she hasn't seen Colton's photo. *Damn Colton.*

Anger greases his synapses and the Merton quote comes to him. "Actions are the doors and windows of being. Unless we act, we have no way of knowing who we are." He rises from the bed, seizes his crutches. Lluvia would want him to reconcile with Thomas, do what he came here to do.

The snow is accumulating quickly, and he doesn't have gloves or a hat, but he is determined now. He should call Noah for assistance, but his urgency and pride prevail, and he places his crutches with deliberation, making his way slowly through the squall which seems on its way to becoming a blizzard.

In the vast, empty residence hall's foyer he shakes the snow off his hair and jacket, the same puffy red jacket he wore in his first months in the monastery that announced him as an outsider. His hands are red and barely functional, his broken tibia aches, but he carries on, pushing through the double door that delivers him to the brothers' chambers. A left turn brings him to the door of Thomas's quarters. A cello is playing in there, the Bach suites. He listens, breathing deeply, suddenly aware of exhaustion. He planned some words but they have evaporated. They weren't an apology as much as a request for détente. *You are dying, let's let the acrimony go.* He waits for his speech to reassemble itself, but exhaustion and cold have blunted his brain. He'll have to improvise.

He knocks. The cello plays on, nimble and flawless. Is that Thomas playing? He knocks again more loudly. The cello continues as the wheelchair whirs into action. The door opens.

"Well, well," Thomas says. "The prodigal son. Come in."

Niall hesitates, overcome: Thomas in his crimson velour bathrobe, a crescendo of the cello's melody, the spectacle of the room with its lavish appointments. Something in his brain snaps audibly.

"What is wrong with you? How can you live like this when everyone else lives in poverty? What makes you think you're so special? And what makes you think you can go into anyone's room and take what you want? It's despicable."

The cello plays on. Thomas watches Niall, his expression blank. Niall crosses the threshold with as much speed as his crutches allow and hobbles to the bookcase on the far side of the room. There it is on the top shelf, *The Solace of Poetry*. He grabs it, wobbles, almost falls.

"This is mine. *Mine.* My mother inscribed it! To me! You have no right to this book. Nor do you have a right to my body. You don't belong here—you're not a believer. You are opportunistic and entitled. Not to mention crazy. I know you're dying, but that doesn't change what I'm saying."

Thomas has rolled himself to the center of the room as if to block Niall's exit. The cello comes to its denouement, stops. In the silence that follows Niall hears his own heavy breathing.

"Are you done?" Thomas asks, cinching the belt of his robe.

Niall says nothing. A few measures of a new piece of music

begin, hip-hop, something Niall's students would know, but Thomas silences it.

"So—you came all the way from New Jersey to yell at me?"

Niall says nothing. The book falls from his grasp, thwacks the floor.

"Look, everything you said—most of it is true. But—" Thomas turns to his lap, shaking his head in a slow metronomic back and forth. He looks back up at Niall. "But *I* am not your problem, Niall. *You* are your problem."

They stare at each other now as if replaying the moments leading up to their fistfight. But now, damaged as they are, there is no way to fight.

Niall goes limp from the depths of his exhaustion. *What is wrong with me?* "I'm sorry." He sighs. "That's not what I came here to say."

Thomas says nothing, rolls to his kitchen, and begins extracting French bread and cold cuts from the refrigerator, erasing Niall with waves of silent disdain. The path to the door now clear, Niall speed-hobbles to the exit.

The snow has intensified, almost blizzard-like, darkening the landscape, making it hard to tell the time of day. He trudges through it step by labored step, knowing it's foolhardy to be out but having no other choice. What is wrong with him that he can't make good on his mission, can't let go of ancient anger? Thomas is dying, for god's sake.

He realizes he left the poetry book on the floor at Thomas's, but he certainly isn't going back. Shapes swarm ahead of him in the eddying snow. Animals? People? Thomas's face—or is it Colton's?— sneering, laughing, mocking him. *I am not your problem, you are your problem. Check your facts, monk-man.* He's losing his bearings, can't continue. He will freeze to death out here like the Little Match Girl from the story his mother used to read him.

He stands on the stoop of his cottage but can't turn the door handle. His gelid hands won't move. What now? His knees buckle. His torso crumples. He stares skyward into the squall, a pointillist's study in white, and his mother's voice comes to him. "The flakes, silver and dark, falling obliquely against the lamplight . . . His soul swooned slowly as he heard the snow falling faintly through the universe and faintly falling, like the descent of their last end, upon all the living and the dead."

He rises, the ecstatic weightlessness of a carnival ride or a human balloon—is this heaven? No, he's being lifted. Noah and someone else. When his vision clears and he comes to consciousness again, he's reclining on the couch, buried under a heap of blankets. Noah lays a heating pad on his belly and hands. Thomas is nearby in his wheelchair watching intently.

"You are one crazy dude," Noah says. "Any longer out there and it might have been lights out. If Thomas hadn't called me . . ."

"You called?" Niall says, his voice a hoarse whisper. Thomas smiles, shrugs. "Thank you."

Noah is putting on his jacket and hat and mittens. "I'm coming back with food and meds. Are you two okay for a bit?"

"We're fine," Thomas says. "Right, Niall?"

Niall nods.

"No going out again," Noah says as he opens the door, letting in a smack of cold wind before stepping out and slamming the door. A vacuum of silence. Thomas and Niall gaze at one another until Niall looks away.

"Are you alright now?" Thomas says. "Warm enough?"

Niall nods. "How did you get here in the snow?"

"My chair is very rugged. Like an all-terrain vehicle." He maneuvers around the coffee table.

"But why are you here after I yelled at you like that?"

"You left your book." Thomas reaches into his bag and plunks the poetry book onto the coffee table. Niall stares at the book. He feels numb, empty of thoughts. He has been without this book for a couple of years now and hasn't really missed it.

"And—I thought, even before you collapsed, that you could probably use some libation." He reaches into his bag again and this time brings out a bottle of whiskey and two glasses. He uncaps it, pours a generous portion into each glass and extends one to Niall.

Niall stares at the amber liquid that flirts with the cabin light, mistrusting its beauty. "I haven't had whiskey since college."

"Go ahead. It won't kill you."

Niall withdraws his hand from under the heating pad and takes the whiskey.

"To us invalids," Thomas says grinning and raising his glass in a toast.

Niall sips and swallows. It burns his throat but fills his chest with a pleasant heat.

"Why are you so angry, Anselm—Niall—whoever you are? Hasn't time addressed your problem with me? There must be other things that are bothering you."

Niall sips his whiskey again, looking out at the snow. He feels Thomas watching him, his expression inexplicably gentle. Like the snow itself falling faintly, faintly falling. It reorders Niall's body, his cells and their mitochondria. He turns to Thomas and weeps.

After a while he finds his voice. "It's complicated."

"No, there you're wrong. It's never as complicated as we want to think it is. It's usually quite simple."

"What is *it*—what are you referring to?"

"Everything."

"You and me?"

"Of course you and me. I wanted to fuck you. And you were scared of me. You refused me. And I was angry. There are more nuances, of course, but those are the basics. Pretty simple."

Thomas downs his glass. "I still love you, just differently. No Eros anymore. No fucking. I'm different."

Really? Niall has never believed that people's essences change, but Thomas does seem different.

"I never wanted sex with you," Niall says. "Do you get that?"

"Sure. But I scared you and you had no idea how to stand up to me. Correct me if I'm wrong."

Niall draws the heating pad from his belly to his chest. His whiskey glass is empty and Thomas refills it before Niall can refuse. Niall sips, hoping to stave off another onslaught of tears, but they arrive anyway, their heat and salt singeing his cheeks. Thank God he's able to cry silently.

"I should tell you I was born a provocateur," Thomas says. "The youngest of five sons. All high achievers. Jerome was the oldest."

"Jerome? I thought he was your uncle."

"Oh yeah, that myth floated around for a while. No, he's my brother. My family was stupidly wealthy. Mainline Philadelphia. And from the get-go I rebelled against all of it. It led to drugs and sex and tangles with the law. I'm sure you heard the rest.

"I know what you're thinking, Niall. I had five years of watching you. You're wondering if I've really changed or if it's just an act, right?"

Niall laughs.

"I know I used to be an asshole. But the world looks different when you know your days are numbered. It depressed me at first. Jerome made me go to a therapist, which was a bust. She wanted me to explore my grief. And I thought, why the fuck should I explore my grief with *her*? I didn't know her from Adam, and she didn't seem that smart. But then she recommended a drug trip. Psilocybin. You might not believe it, but it changed the way I see the world. It really did."

"One trip can change you that much?"

"I can only say what happened to me."

The silence between them now bears none of the ominousness of their previous silences, it moves like a stream and carries the restorative quality of a deep breath. Niall's eyes close. He's drunk and drowsy and spent from emoting.

"I've always thought of you as a good man, but much too scared for your own good. What is making you so angry? It can't really be me, is it?"

Niall opens his eyes and tries to rally. He wants it to be simple, but it still feels complicated. He repositions himself so he can see Thomas more directly. Scrawny, blue-eyed, black-bearded Thomas.

"I have a student—he's giving me trouble. A provocateur, I guess I'd call him."

"Provocative teenagers are the worst."

"He's rich and smug."

Thomas laughs. "Do you mean to be describing me? Maybe there's hope for him too."

Niall chuckles. He wishes Thomas could see Colton and then deliver an opinion. It would take more words than he can now summon to render the situation accurately. Maybe tomorrow. For now the danger has passed and he can let himself sleep.

40

Bells ring, a dreamlike choir. He floats into consciousness, opens his eyes, unsure where he is. Sunlight fills both windows, illuminates pillows of snow, sparking blue and silver. Snow fairies. Pixies. Where is Liam? In a brain movie that takes seconds he arrives back in adulthood, a student of history, a monk, a teacher. His gaze assembles the room slowly: the strange bed he is in, crutches leaning against the headboard, the couch, the coffee table, the bottle of whiskey on the table. Thomas was here. They drank whiskey together. No wonder he is so dazed. But he has no headache, none of the usually signs of a hangover. Judging from the look of the sunlight he has slept until midday.

He sits, props himself up with pillows, questions flooding his brain. How much whiskey did they drink? Who moved him from couch to bed? What did he say to Thomas? The bells are tapering off now, their final notes still bouncing on the air, spectral, as if all the monastery's former residents are tiptoeing inside them. He feels Francis's presence, misses him acutely. He remembers snippets of the Poe poem his mother used to read him. "Keeping time, time, time. / In a song of a Runic rhyme . . . the bells, bells, bells, bells / bells, bells, bells." How he would like to get himself to the chapel if only to listen to the brothers chanting together, bonded, entangled in a love beyond words. A love like the basketball players, not sexual, but intensely physical. He thinks of trying to get himself there now, but it would take him forever on his crutches in the snow. He would arrive late and draw attention, and that is the last thing he wants. He seizes his phone, dials Lluvia before rationality can tell him it's a bad idea.

"It's me. Please pick up." But she doesn't.

Noah has left a breakfast of eggs and toast that has gone cold. His mother has left a message. Weather permitting, she will come for him tomorrow; the roads should be clear by then. The message pops him awake. He has to finish his conversation with Thomas before he leaves. Thomas might have more to say about Colton. If only he had a copy of the photo. Trinity said it's gone viral on social media but Niall isn't on those sites. As he is thinking of this, he sees a text from Trinity. It must have come while he was sleeping. As if she has read his mind, there is the photo. What a good friend she is.

He enlarges the image, examining its details. When Colton first showed it to him in the hallway, he saw Trinity's extravagant laugh, her head thrown back, mouth open, his own tamer smile. But now he notices how his body is twisted a bit and leaning toward hers so their shoulders almost touch. It announces loudly that he is her admirer and acolyte. It's easy to see, as he thought the first time, that people might think they were lovers. What limited imagination most people have that they cannot picture a friendship like his and Trinity's.

He thanks her in a quick text, distracted by the thought of Lluvia seeing the photo. That's how the world works. He can't prevent it. Let it go. If he and Lluvia were together it would matter, but now it shouldn't matter. Yet it matters. He places another call to her. "Please." But she doesn't pick up.

He thinks of the day he deserted her to go to Manhattan with Trinity. What was he thinking? She deserved a better explanation for his difficulty committing, a real conversation of some kind, not deflection. He can still hear the sound of her weeping on his voicemail, her oceanic sighs. How he wishes he had done things differently. *I miss you*, he writes in a text. It's a bad idea, but he sends it anyway.

Over a foot of snow has fallen, recoloring the monastery grounds from autumn brown to winter white. Over a foot of snow has fallen, but the paths have been shoveled and sanded. A few brothers are still working on the parking lot, their white robes fluttering past the drifts so they are almost indistinguishable from the landscape. Simon and Joseph approach from the opposite direction, hailing him, their cheeks red from the cold and exertion and high spirits.

"Anselm! Good afternoon!"

"Hey," he says, "the snow is beautiful." But what he wants to say from under his heavy cloak of longing is: *You are beautiful. I miss you all.*

A fire crackles in Thomas's quarters. Niall settles in. He hasn't been in front of a fire since his childhood.

"The whiskey didn't do you in?" Thomas says.

"I'm a bit dazed, but otherwise fine. Did you mean to leave it with me?"

"Keep it. I have plenty more."

Niall lays his phone on the shelf of Thomas's wheelchair, open to the photo of him and Trinity.

"What does this say to you?"

Thomas enlarges the photo. "Good friends having fun."

"Nothing more?"

"I don't think so. Who is she? Why do you ask?"

Niall says everything he can think of to say about Colton—and his friendship with Trinity and breakup with Lluvia. Thomas remains silent, rolls himself to the fire, and stabs the logs with an iron poker that falls from his grasp and clatters on the stone hearth.

"We need Noah for this," he says, "I'm not strong enough." He rolls back closer to the couch where Niall sits. "I could laugh but I won't because you might take it wrong. This is exactly the kind of thing I might have done as a teenager to taunt one of my teachers."

"Really?"

"I told you I was a provocateur."

"Yes, but . . ."

Noah knocks and enters with a rolling cart of food.

"I have lunch for both of you."

"How did you know I'd be here?" Niall says.

Noah smiles. "I'm an observant guy."

White bean soup and grilled cheese sandwiches. Salad and grapes and oat bars and hot tea. Massive quantities of everything.

"Stay and eat with us," Thomas urges Noah, who hesitates only briefly before agreeing. "And we need you to fix the fire for us weaklings." They divide the food three ways. Niall is famished, eats everything including half of Thomas's sandwich.

Thomas laughs. "A man with an appetite like yours doesn't belong here."

"But I miss it. I never thought I would."

"Really? You don't want to come back, do you?

Niall thinks. At moments there is nothing he wants more. The clarity of life here. The silence. The community.

"It's a kind of utopia," he says.

Thomas regards him. "Do you really mean that?"

"Well—"

"What do you think, Noah?" Thomas says. "Is this a utopia?"

Noah lays down his soup spoon. "I'm too new to say, I think. I went to the commune because I thought it was a utopia. And then . . ."

The fire crackles. The half-burned logs tumble into dozens of embers that glow like eyes with things to say.

"Exactly," Thomas says.

"Probably the only utopia is where you're going," Noah says to

Thomas. "I almost envy you. But I'd miss the food." He holds up the last bits of his sandwich, and they all laugh.

"Maybe this isn't a perfect utopia," Niall says, "but it's a working community, and it's about as good as human beings can do."

"But you left," Thomas says. Retina-to-retina, unswerving, they regard each other. Dueling—but gently.

"Yes," Niall says, "I was immature."

41

Moonlight pools on the snow, a full moon, silvery-white. They shuffle along the path to vespers silenced by the summoning bells, which are in themselves a kind of silence. A triumvirate: Thomas in the lead, behind him Niall, Noah last, spotting Niall. At the front door they converge with the other brothers. Abbot Jerome, Joseph and Simon and Stephen and all the others, everyone nodding, smiling their welcomes. *Silence is our mother tongue*, the Abbot used to say.

Candlelight dances everywhere, a ritual of the Advent season. Niall had forgotten, along with so much else he's forgotten, how otherworldly it is. The way the flames flirt with the stained glass, cast light in hidden places, and bend in all directions as if dancing with each other. He used to love Advent, all its rituals and the anticipation of newness.

The Abbot insists they sit up front to one side where they can be seen. Niall has no idea what the Abbot's purpose is, but he is glad to be where he can see them all, alike in their robes as a flock of birds of a similar feather, but different too. He can never say for sure which is more important, their similarities or differences.

The organ plays: another thing he'd forgotten. "Oh come, oh come, Emmanuel and ransom captive Israel . . ." How did he not appreciate this organ, its velvet cascade of sound billowing and warm, rising to the ceiling and enfolding them in its crescendos as irresistibly as love?

42

His mother comes for him the following day. Niall will return for his car at New Year when he can drive. Jerome and Thomas and Noah and Joseph have gathered in the parking lot to bid him goodbye. They all seem high-spirited, almost bouncy. They introduce themselves to his mother. Noah hands her a brown bag with two rounds of the monastery's cheese and two loaves of whole grain bread.

"We thought you would enjoy this over the holidays," the Abbot says.

"Oh my, thank you so much," she says. "They're heavy!"

"We're trying to fatten you up," Thomas says.

They laugh and embrace, his mother included.

Niall watches the brothers recede in his side view mirror, sees the fraternal resemblance between Jerome and Thomas, the full beards, the cocked heads, the matching smiles. An indistinct longing fills him again.

"What nice men," his mother says. "I knew they had to be nice, but it's good to finally see it."

The Mohawk Trail takes them past woods and pastures and small towns along the Deerfield River. Snow drifts diminish the already narrow roads, so Eva drives at a cautious, meditative pace and Niall takes in the landscape, seeing these places he has only zipped past before. He has missed New England. Even without talking he feels close to his mother.

"So?" Eva says.

"So what?"

"What took you there again? You're not going back are you?"

They're passing the yard of a ranch house where an inflatable Santa has popped and sagged into the snow, still smiling and waving.

Niall chuckles. "No, I'm not going back."

"But you thought of it?"

"Maybe. But only very briefly. I went to see Thomas, who's dying of ALS."

"I wondered." She shakes her head. "Poor man."

"Yes, poor man. But he's a better man too, now that he's facing death."

"How long does he have?"

"I don't know. I didn't ask."

"Oh, Niall."

They've arrived at Route 91 which will take them south to Route 2 which will speed them east to Boston. The sudden presence of so many other cars makes Niall feel he has arrived at a dinner party. He preferred the slow intimacy of the back roads.

"There's something I've been meaning to tell you," Eva says. "I should have told you sooner, but I worried it might upset you."

He waits. She pulls into the right lane and slows a little.

A quick glance. "Lluvia and I have been getting to know each other."

He waits.

"She called me. She wanted to know more about you, why you would leave so suddenly without explanation. And why you kept saying you were a terrible person. She thought you might have secrets that would explain it."

He waits, fixing his gaze on the white line to regulate himself.

"Anyway, we had a few long conversations—not just about you, but about her past and my past. And, you know, Life. I found her to be so easy to talk to. So open and so wise really. So I invited her and Flora to visit. We had a wonderful time. Flora is exceptional.

"I knew you wouldn't like this. But, honestly, you relinquished the chance to have a say when you broke up with her. She and I have a relationship now that is independent of you."

He closes his eyes, trying to picture Lluvia and Flora in his mother's apartment. What would they do on a visit together? More importantly, what would they talk about? He'd like to ask if Lluvia mentioned the photo of him and Trinity, but to ask such a question would seem to imply he and Trinity were doing something wrong. Everything his mother says about Lluvia is true, but do they really need to be friends?

He and Eva don't talk for the rest of the drive home. The speed of the car and the relentless racket of its engine turns anger to envy then sadness. It's a relief to arrive at her building where he stumps up the stairs to her second floor apartment and retires to her guest room, all the jubilance he felt during the goodbyes at the monastery drained.

The remaining days of December at his mother's apartment are quiet. She has two and a half weeks off, and they spend most of their time in the living room reading and talking about everything but Lluvia. Niall notices a Christmas card from Lluvia amidst his mother's display. It features a beaming mermaid emerging from the ocean garbed in red holiday sparkle. *Peace* it says across the top, and inside, *Love, Lluvia and Flora. So glad we've met.*

They take short walks to strengthen Niall's leg, and they cook, Niall attentive to her techniques, determined to develop some kitchen skills. They've agreed not to exchange Christmas gifts, but they decorate a small Christmas tree mounted on a table.

His mother drives him to a few physical therapy appointments which makes him feel like a child again, comfortable and safe. He feels a surge of contentment being there with her.

But he notices she seems wistful, and when he questions her she says it makes her sad that she'll never really know her sons again the way she knew them when they were boys.

"You were so transparent back then. Especially you. You told me everything. Now I really know nothing about your life."

"But I've told you so much. What else would you like to know? Ask me anything."

"No, Niall. You know you don't want me to do that."

He hates to admit she's right.

"I will say one thing though. I might be overstepping, but I'm sorry that—"

"Please don't."

They fall silent. He thinks about how few words it takes to inflict harm. His mother brushes back her hair and looks out the window.

"I guess you mean Lluvia?"

"Yes."

43

When Niall suggests going to Christmas Mass, his mother frowns.

"How about a walk instead?"

He is agreeable but is surprised when she drives them to Mount Auburn Cemetery. He has only been here once long ago when he was very young, but she apparently comes here frequently. It's her favorite place to walk.

They set out on a paved path that goes slightly uphill into the cemetery's interior and away from the mayhem of Cambridge traffic. Something in the air announces Christmas Day, even after the carols at the entrance have faded into the distance. It's the unblemished snow and the wintry-blue light of mid-afternoon and a clarity in the air that makes Niall feel he can see a great distance. Some of the broad-branching maples are as impressive as the monuments and the roads and paths are pleasingly curved. It is obvious that someone put some effort into designing the place. A few small birds hop about in the snow.

"This is a favorite place for many people to go birding," Eva says.

"That's hard to imagine."

"You wouldn't say that in the spring or summer. Even now birds are out there. They're just in hiding."

On cue more birds appear, landing on all the flat surfaces of one of the most imposing monuments like decoration.

"Juncos, I think," Eva says. "I'm just learning."

They walk slowly, more like monks than civilians. His mother hums. He had forgotten this habit of hers he loved so much as a child, tuneless melodies that told him she was happy.

Bigelow, Aldrich, Eddy, Peabody, Agassi, Howe, Holmes. He recognizes these names of prominent Bostonians without knowing exactly who they are.

"1830–1869, 1840–1898, 1865–1925," he reads.

"I sometimes feel ambivalent about coming here," his mother says. "It's mostly so many white men who wielded power and their undersung wives. But there are some wonderful women buried here too. Margaret Fuller, Julia Ward Howe, Amy Lowell. Did you ever read Amy Lowell's poem 'Patterns'? Maybe I read it to you? Or maybe not. It's quite an intense poem. A feminist poem. 'I walk down the patterned garden paths / In my stiff brocaded gown. / With my powdered hair and jeweled fan, / I too am a rare / Pattern. As I wander down / The garden paths.' I read that poem and am so glad I was born when I was born."

"I don't remember that poem."

"She won the Pulitzer Prize posthumously."

"Oh."

"And she was a lesbian."

"Oh. Was she related to Robert Lowell?"

"Not directly, but same family."

They detour off the main artery onto one of the smaller paths. Brewster Brigham, Cabot. Such WASPy names.

"I bet there are many racists here," he says.

"Of course. Many abolitionists, and many racists. Side by side everywhere, even today."

The uncleared snow beneath their feet is slippery. By mutual silent accord they stop and stare down the hill. All these dead people. So much history. So many lives with passions and sorrows, good deeds and bad. He feels a quivering beneath his feet, radiating up his shins. A humming. A silent song. A prayer. What are they saying to him? They know things he is just beginning to learn. What are they telling him to do?

Two crows interrupt the silence, swooping down from a maple tree and landing on top of one of the humbler gravestones. His mother turns to him and smiles.

44

His first night back in New Jersey, the day before school will begin, he lies in bed in the dark, wide awake. His phone lies beside him pathetically quiet. When he was in Massachusetts he must have called Lluvia at least a dozen times, and she never picked up. He is too proud to call yet again.

Trinity answers on the first ring. "I thought you'd call. You're back home?"

Home? Where is home?

"Yes, I'm home."

"You ready for tomorrow?"

"It's Colton Day."

"What is that supposed to mean?"

"I'm going to fix things."

"It's about time. You give that boy way too much power."

"Do people still think we're a couple?"

"Probably. But so what?"

He laughs. "I would love to take a class of yours."

"Really? Math?"

"No—Life."

45

As soon as he steps into the school lobby, students stream past him with the chutzpah of Bastille-stormers, some of them calling out his name, some of them pausing to high-five.

"O'Malley! *Que paso?*"

"You're back!"

"*Que lo que, hermano!*"

"Mr. O, how's the leg?"

Some of these students who greet him he doesn't even know, but apparently they know him, the Prodigal Son. It never occurred to him that his absence would be noted by students he doesn't teach. It makes him irrationally happy, and he sails through his morning classes, loving his students and telling them about visiting Mount Auburn Cemetery, how he felt its history radiating under his feet. They kid him, "You're a nut, Mr. O."

After lunch his nerves kick in. He sits at his desk awaiting his fifth period students. He stands. He sits again. He thinks about Thomas telling him Colton is a provocateur, nothing more.

They arrive en masse, a swarm of his favorite students. Jayden and Rania. Dominic and Anthony. Tiffany and Aliyah and Camilla. Mateo trailing behind. They crowd in, groaning and laughing, plying him with greetings. *Yo, Mr. O! Hey, dude! Watsup bro? My man!*

"We thought you might not come back," Rania says.

"Why would you think that?"

"Someone said you were going to be a monk again."

"Who said that?"

No one knows. "Well, it's not true. Look, I'm here, aren't I?" He looks around at their active faces, his eyes are tearing—he wishes he didn't have to teach.

They chitchat about the holidays. Colton is late. The students ask about his leg, and he tells them the "official" story that he took a bad fall on the ice, drawing it out, embellishing it for drama. He isn't funny, but they laugh anyway. It seems as if they like him more than before.

"Where's Colton?" he finally asks as casually as he can.

"He's outta here," Jayden says. "Gone to some other school."

"Another school? Where? Why?"

"Go figure," Jayden says.

"Good riddance," says Rania.

Niall has no idea what to say—or even what to feel. Relief, yes, but now how can he make amends? Hopelessly distracted, he tries to corral the students' attention, as well as his own, to the subject matter at hand, the lead-up to World War I.

"Do we still have to do our research papers?" Dominic asks. A surprising question coming from a student who pays little attention to his work.

"Only if you want extra credit. We're moving on to catch up with the curriculum."

"World War I is boring," Tiffany says, regarding him seductively from under her veil of hair, her tone begging.

"I'll do my best to make it interesting."

"Isn't there more to history than wars?" Rania says. "I swear, we go from the Civil War to World War I. Then World War II, right? And then probably the Cold War. Then Vietnam. Iraq. Ukraine. On and on, wars forever. I think there's more to history than just wars."

He takes in Rania's vermillion head scarf, her furrowed brow. He can imagine her holding public office someday, speaking her mind. How right she is—history is so much more than wars.

46

Niall wakes to the snowstorm he hoped wouldn't happen. More than a foot has fallen on top of the old snow, and it's still coming down. School has been canceled, routine smashed. It's a pain, but an undeniably beautiful pain, whitewashing the urban dirt and instilling in him a spirit of adventure. He remembers the snowstorms of his childhood when school was canceled and his mother would take him and Liam out on walks to the park. They would make snowmen and snowballs and snow angels, and back at home they'd "sugar-off," pouring hot maple syrup over bowls of snow and watching it harden into candy.

By early afternoon the roads have been plowed, and someone has shoveled a path from his building to the street, so he pays a neighbor kid to shovel out his car and he ventures out, driving at fifteen miles an hour up and down the residential streets, watching kids who are out doing exactly what he did as a kid, the adults around them dutifully shoveling.

He comes to a larger thoroughfare he doesn't recognize, strip malls on either side. He turns onto it hesitantly. Salt and sand have turned the snow to thick slush that causes him to skid; his tires aren't equipped for snow. He shouldn't be out here, driving at this scaredy-cat pace, cars honking and zipping around him. He turns into one of the strip malls, trying to calculate how best to reverse his direction. He parks in front of a Starbucks, a liquor store next to it. Both are open. People crave coffee and alcohol on days like this.

He suddenly thinks he'd like to get drunk, feel alcohol streaming through his blood as it did with Thomas, that glittery loosening of thoughts. He will get drunk and raise a toast to the new, kinder Thomas.

The store, small and dark and empty but for the clerk, is crammed from floor to ceiling with booze. He asks where the whiskey is, trying to remember the brand Thomas served him. The clerk, a morose middle-aged white man immersed in his phone, directs him to the back of the store, and Niall limps down the aisle, the astringent scent of cold and alcohol biting the air. He squeezes past a stack of cartons waiting to be unpacked. The back wall is devoted to whiskey—who knew there were so many brands? Another patron is there too, examining the offerings, pulling down bottles and reading the labels then restoring them to the shelf.

"I'm trying to remember the name of a very good whiskey I had recently," Niall says, "but I can't remember for the life of me. Would you be able to point me to some good ones?"

It isn't his habit to initiate conversation with strangers, but a storm like this alters habits. The man turns his attention from the shelf to Niall. He's a young man—a boy really, probably not old enough to buy alcohol—wearing a black leather jacket. Blue eyes, shaggy black hair. He's not someone Niall knows, but the man/boy seems to recognize him.

"Don't say anything." The man/boy gestures to the front of the store.

The voice. "Colton?"

He nods. The dark hair has transformed him, but the voice is the same. Ambushed, Niall feels clammy, sick to his stomach. "I didn't think I'd see you again," he says, trying to sound neutral. "I heard you were leaving."

Colton smiles. "Yeah. I'm flying to California tomorrow, so . . ."

"That sounds nice."

"Maybe. Maybe not. New school—we'll see." He looks down at the bottle he's holding, stroking it like a genie.

"You don't want to stay here?"

"Fuck no. Too many people here hate me. You included. Right?"

"I misjudged you. And I'm very sorry about that. I leapt to conclusions."

"Well, I'm writing my next paper on *habeas corpus*." He looks up from his bottle. "You know, *innocent until proven guilty*."

"Seriously?"

"A joke, Mr. O'Malley. A joke. You probably didn't think I knew what *habeas corpus* meant did you?"

"You dyed your hair."

"Observant of you."

"Why?"

"Why do you think?" He turns away from Niall and pulls back the collar of his jacket to expose his bare shoulder. The tattoo is gone, leaving the skin chafed and red. "So there you go—I told you I was going to . . ."

"Look, I hope you're not leaving the school because of me."

Colton's expression changes to something that might be surprise. "If that's what you really think . . ." He shakes his head and readjusts his jacket and glances nervously toward the front of the store.

"Is that a good brand you've got there?"

"Good enough."

"I'll get it for you."

Colton hands the bottle to Niall as if he expected this all along, as if he is owed it. Niall takes one of the same brand for himself. The floor creaks beneath their boots synchronously, like a kind of music, making the walk feel ceremonial as they return to the front of the store. Niall lays the two bottles of whiskey on the counter. The clerk looks up from his phone and assesses Colton but says nothing.

"Is the snow good or bad for business?" Niall asks.

"Bad. Always bad."

The bill comes to two hundred and sixty-six dollars. Niall tries not to gasp. Alcohol for rich men like Colton and Thomas, not for men on a teacher's salary.

Niall walks Colton to his car, the black BMW, and hands him his bottle. Colton nods.

"I actually like the snow," Niall says as Colton slides into the driver's seat, salutes, and pulls out fast, joining the flow of traffic.

When Niall returns home the snow is still coming down, but lazily, sleepily. The expedition has exhausted him. It's only three o'clock in the afternoon, but who cares, he pours himself a glass of whiskey, wishing Lluvia were here. He stretches out on the couch with a blanket and pillows, positioning himself so he can watch the snow through the window threading its way through the leafless branches of the maple tree. His lids close and open as he sips and watches. Someone can see God out there in the flakes and tree branches and nimbus clouds, even if Niall can't. Maybe buying whiskey for Colton meant more to the boy than an extended apology would have. How badly he has underestimated Colton. As Thomas pointed out, he is still a teenager, for god's sake; he has years ahead of him to change.

In the midst of the flakes an image of Thomas forms. He's in his wheelchair, the only color is his blue eyes, swirled like marbles. All his personhood is packed into those complicated eyes, all his struggling soul. Is Thomas a good person now? Good like Niall's mother is good, like Lluvia is good, good like Francis? What is goodness? *Please forgive me, Thomas.* Niall thinks of Merton: "We can go out to them without vanity and without complacency, loving them with something of the purity and gentleness and hiddenness of God's love for us."

As Niall's lids finally droop into sleep, Merton is still with him: *It's all a matter of staying awake.*

47

An email comes from the Abbot on a Sunday in early March. *Thomas has passed away.* Niall stares at his screen, temporarily frozen as he takes in the next words. *I am sorry to have to tell you he took his own life. We all mourn.*

The day started out sunny and warm for March, but by afternoon a light drizzle has moved in, sending most people inside. He parks in a public lot near the boardwalk, descends to the beach and heads south, his eye on the weather fronts battling over the water, swaths of blue up high, swaths of gray closer to the horizon. Rania's question from months ago has been framing his outlook ever since. *Isn't there more to history than war?* He wanted to reassure her, to say: *Yes, Rania, of course.* But there's little evidence for that—war has been a dominant force, casting its shadow over everything for centuries, millennia. Even the forces of weather are always skirmishing, just like the seagulls, squirrels, animals of all species, including the human animal. Rania herself is probably waging some battle she's hardly aware of.

After walking two miles or so, he turns and heads north again, the Manhattan skyline in his sightlines now. He and Trinity will be going to an art exhibition there next weekend, to see the work of another college friend of hers. Of course Thomas would find a way to end his own life if he wished to do so.

He's almost back to where he began when he notices someone

swimming, stroking south parallel to the shoreline. He stops to watch, impressed by any person who is unperturbed by the cold water, the overcast skies and drizzle. The water's surface, however, is calm, perfect for swimming. It's a woman he sees, as the swimmer turns and strokes north, the bare arms slim. As she passes him, continuing north, his vision seems to sharpen, and he recognizes Lluvia. The head and hair and arms, all hers. She wears goggles but no bathing cap. It's not surprising to see her here, lover of swimming that she is. He waves madly but, head down, she doesn't see.

He can't turn away now, desperate for her to notice him. She dives under and makes another turn, heading south again, raising her head momentarily to get her bearings.

Frantic to be seen, he pulls off his shoes and socks, his rain jacket, his shirt and trousers. Everything but his boxers. He races to the water's edge, overrides the shock of the water's chill, dives in and thrashes toward her. Now that he's in the water she seems farther away. He's a clumsy swimmer, can only make himself go so fast.

"Lluvia!" he calls, inhaling water, choking. "Lluvia, it's me! Wait! Lluvia!"

She doesn't hear—or doesn't respond—continues swimming.

"Lluvia," he bellows.

She lifts her head again, still seems not to see him. He swims with his face down for added speed, but he's out of practice, and a rhythm evades him—he was never a good swimmer in the first place. He comes up for air and treads water, gasping hands numb, watching her in hopes she'll be stopped by the force of his gaze.

Then he doubts himself—it isn't Lluvia. This woman is bigger than Lluvia, her hair darker. His frantic heart plummets in disappointment. But he continues to watch, hoping the power of his gaze might turn her into Lluvia again. He's willing to wait for such a transformation. He blinks hard, swims as fast as he can though he'll never keep pace with her. *"Let me see, then, the gift of silence, and poverty and solitude, where everything I touch is turned into prayer: where the sky is my prayer, the birds are my prayer, the wind in the trees is my prayer, for God is all in all."* This woman, whoever she is, is his prayer. The water-darkened hair, the capable arms, someone crazy enough to be swimming in March in the rain.

He calls out again, using all his reserves. "LLU-VI-A!"

His strength is waning, the cold sapping him quickly. If he swims out farther he won't be able to return to shore. But he can't peel his eyes from the swimmer. He swirls his arms and legs, a human quadrapus, trying to stay afloat. Eventually this woman will come up for air again and see him, recognize him. *Please let it be Lluvia.*

If he's a good man, a man who can stay awake, she might turn, swim toward him, eager, smiling, pausing to wave. *Please, please, swim to me.*

Acknowledgements

On January 2, 2023, Cai died of ALS, invoking the Death with Dignity laws of Oregon, where she lived. The morning of her death, she submitted the just-completed manuscript of *The Bells* to her agent. All through the two years of her illness, she worked on this novel (under the working title *Dual, Duel*), unable to speak and barely able to write (she always wrote longhand). She never allowed her body's deterioration to deter her from her main purpose in life, which was to write.

Cai had no idea whether *The Bells* would be published. She didn't have time to dedicate the book to a specific person or select a fitting epigraph. Those tasks fell to me, her husband. And now the task of thanking the people who helped her complete this book falls to me as well. She left no notes about who to thank. I'll name just a few.

Thanks to Miriam Gershow, to whom I've dedicated the book, as Cai herself might have done. Miriam was steadfast in treating Cai how she wanted, as a regular person, the same person she'd always been, throughout the progression of her illness. Miriam was co-conspirator in the scheme to rob impending death of its power to diminish Cai's power, its insidious goal of belittling the magnificent woman Cai was.

Thanks to two of Cai's main champions, Deborah Schneider and Kate Gale, her agent and publisher, respectively. Both of these women read the book after Cai had died and decided to move forward with publishing it. Cai loved and appreciated them very much, as do I.

Thanks to the wonderful journalist and friend Lorraine Berry, who reviewed Cai's books and wrote eloquently about Cai's life. And to Sandra Luckow, who committed Cai's journey to film.

Ben Howorth, Cai's son, and her family and friends, too numerous to name, deserve enormous thanks for supporting Cai on the path to her final transition.

Of course, Cai would have thanked me, not only for being her caregiver for the last two years of her life, but forever and always being her first reader, her writing partner, though we never wrote anything of note together. I didn't and don't need any thanks for that. The privilege of being Cai's first reader and creative confidante is still one of the greatest gifts of my life.

I will always thank her for it.

—Paul Calandrino

Biographical Note

Cai Emmons was the author of six novels: *This Mother's Son*, *The Stylist*, *Weather Woman*, *Sinking Islands*, *Livid*, and *Unleashed*, and one short story collection, *Vanishing*. Winner of the Oregon Book Award, the Leapfrog Press Fiction Contest, a Nautilus Award, and finalist for the *Missouri Review* Editor's Prize as well as the *Narrative Magazine* Fiction Prize, Emmons was also short-listed for the Sarton Award and nominated for a Pushcart Prize. Her essays and stories appeared in such publications as *TriQuarterly*, *LitHub*, *Electric Literature*, *The LA Times*, and *Ms. Magazine*. A *summa cum laude* graduate of Yale College, Emmons held MFA degrees in film and fiction. She taught at several colleges and universities, most recently in the University of Oregon's Creative Writing Program. After living with ALS for two years, she ended her life using Oregon's Death with Dignity laws in January 2023.

www.ingramcontent.com/pod-product-compliance
Lightning Source LLC
Chambersburg PA
CBHW031213260626
47169CB00007B/2040